MENDING HEARTS

Sincere Robinson

BLUE KNIGHT STORIES

Jacksonville, FL

I want to dedicate this book to my parents who worked to ensure that I could live out my dreams. To my family who gave me the motivation to keep fighting for what I believed in. Finally, to Rachel Renee Griggs who believed in my work and gave me the push to keep writing. I am truly humbled and thankful to have been blessed with so many great people in my life.

Forward

I pulled Cyan down with me as shots rang through the air, then I sat there and watched my brand-new Beamer as it sped off. I got up with a laugh of disgust because all I had was a flesh wound and the only thing that I lost was my car, so I thought. As I looked down and saw my stomach bleeding, I said, *"Man this is nothing, "* but suddenly everything changed. I turned to check on Cyan and tears filled my eyes as I saw my fiancée lying on the ground, covered in blood.

ONE

It all began on a bright and sunny Friday afternoon. I called Cyan on the phone and I told her I wanted to take her out. I went to her house and talked to her parents while I waited for her to finish getting ready. As I spoke to her parents, I glanced up and saw Cyan walking down the steps. She was amazingly beautiful: 5'7", bluish – green eyes, caramel complexion, long, beautiful, flowing black hair with brown highlights, a nice shape and a beautiful smile that made my heart leap! Just one look and you would think that she was a model. Yeah, that was my queen. She was wearing a pair of blue skinny jeans with a black shirt that complimented her assets very nicely. We said our goodbyes to her parents, went outside and got into my brand-new black BMW. Staring into her eyes made me feel like I was in Aruba swimming in the beautiful, sparkling ocean. It was so easy to get lost in her eyes. I started daydreaming about our date last night. It was at the Diamond Club, a club that my brother Quinton (everyone called him Q) and Cyan's cousin Esco owned. I told Cyan to invite her friends and meet us at the club; it had been a month since I last seen her, she had gone to North Carolina to visit family.

The Diamond Club was a very classy, upscale type of club. If you were not invited, you could not get in. There was a stairway and elevator that led to five different floors. Each floor had different rooms that played different types of music. I decided to meet Cyan on the main floor because I wanted to hook up in the R&B room. The rooms on the main floor played Hip-Hop, Rap, and R&B. The D.J. in the R&B room was playing mostly slow jams all night. The rooms on the second floor played Reggae, Techno, and Pop. The third floor played Old-School Jams, Disco, and Country. The fourth floor of the club had offices and conference rooms. The fifth floor was the newest edition; it was called the Red-Light Special Floor which had three private rooms for Quinton, Esco, and I. Each room had a designated key and they could only be accessed through the el-evators.

My boys spotted Cyan's friends so that let me know she was somewhere in the room. I went and sat at a booth in the corner, looking around trying to find Cyan at a table, booth, dance floor, or wherever. I really needed to see her; my heart was racing. I was so excited, but I tried to remain cool and calm. I checked my watch. It was 10:00 P.M. and I thought,

"We've been in the club for 15 minutes, where is Cyan?" Esco came up to me and said, *"What up Sin?"* *"What up Esco?"* He smiled and said, *"You saw Cyan yet?"* *"Na man, where is she?"* *"She's over there in a booth waiting for you."* He pointed to the booth where she was sitting. I looked over and saw her. It was like everything was moving in slow motion and almost came to a complete stop. There was Cyan sitting in the booth, sipping on a drink and wearing a red and black dress with her hair up in a sexy bun, makeup light but enhancing her natural beauty, black Jimmy Choo heels drawing more attention to her mile-long sexy legs. "How did I miss her?" It was like she was in her own little world; her eyes were closed, and she was swaying slowly to the music. As she opened her eyes, they met mine, she gave me that same little smile that she always gave me whenever she saw me. She looked so beautiful. I sat back and just gave a grin and thought to myself, that sexy shorty over there is all mine. *"Wow, after all these years my cousin still takes your breath away huh?"* I woke up out of my little daydream and answered, *"Esco, you have no idea, man."* *"Go get her Sin."* *"No doubt, you don't have to tell me twice."* Esco walked away. I got up and walked over to Cyan's table. I put my hand out; she took it and got up. I spun her around, checking her out from head

to toe and gave her a hug and a soft passionate kiss. I took her out to the dance floor as *"I Wanna Love You"* by Donnell Jones started playing. I pulled Cyan close to me and said, *"Baby, I love you so much."* I kissed her on the cheek as she told me she loved me. She was holding me so tight. I kept thinking to myself, I don't want this night to end.

Cyan and I danced to slow jam after slow jam. I looked into her eyes and said, *"Baby, I want you."* She looked at me, bit her lip and said, *"I want you too."* I took her by the hand, and we started to leave the room. I took Cyan to the elevator and we entered it. I pulled her close to me and started kissing her as the doors closed. I inserted my key into the keyhole that was marked Red-Light Special and we were on our way up. We reached the fifth floor in no time. We stepped out of the elevator and started walking down the long hallway that was lined with the Red-Light Special rooms. We walked down to the room that had a gold plate on the door with Sincere engraved into it.

I unlocked the door and we walked into a medium sized room that had a dim red glow to it. There was a soft circle chair with a backrest in the middle of the floor and there was also a bed up against the wall, just in case I got too intoxicated or wanted to spend some "quality time" with Cyan. I turned on the stereo system with the remote and immediately *"I Can't Wait"* by Avant started playing. Cyan sat me down on the chair. She started to kiss me. I slipped her shoulder straps down to her arms, not exposing her breasts too much, well not yet at least. I started to kiss Cyan on her neck as she started to unbutton my shirt. She started running her fingers up and down my chest and began kissing me on my neck as I started feeling on her butt through her dress.

"You're wearing my favorite, aren't you? Mmmmhmmmm...Somebody had plans tonight," I whispered into Cyan's ear. *"You have no idea,"* she softly whispered into my ear and then went on to say, *"What are you waiting for?"* I slipped her dress up as she started unzipping my pants.

I slowly lifted Cyan up and turned her around placing her on the chair. Just then *"Somebody's Gotta Be On Top"* by Joe started playing. I put Cyan's legs up over my shoulders and started kissing her thighs and moved down in between her legs. Cyan started moaning and pushed my face into her warm, moist lake of love. She grabbed me by my head and started to wind and grind on my face. We both started getting turned on and feeling like we were in ecstasy. Cyan pulled my head up and looked me in my eyes and started giggling. She bit her lip and motioned for me to come to her. We both got up;

she sat me down and lifted her dress so she could get on top of me again. She pulled my nature out and started rubbing and grinding on it. She slowly moved up and as she did, I unsnapped her thong and then she slowly came down on my nature allowing it to enter her. As it did, she let out a soft moan and grabbed me tightly. She was holding my neck real tight as she moved her hips back and forth. She was moving around as if she was giving me a striptease and all I could tell myself was, *"This is the greatest sex that I have ever had."* Cyan slowly leaned back as I held her and we both made motions as if we were doing a slow wind together to the beat of the music. She started moaning and pushed me back as she started to climax. She grabbed on to me tighter and tighter and started moving faster and faster until she finished. I felt her juices starting to flow down on me.

"I love you so much baby," Cyan said half speaking, half moaning. *"I love you too girl,"* I replied. I grabbed Cyan's butt tighter and started caressing it as I pushed deeper into her. She gently pushed my head down to her breasts and I started sucking on her now hard nipples. I don't discriminate and I didn't want to spoil one nipple, so I moved over to the other one and did the same. Cyan started softly scratching my head with her nails, then pulled my head up and looked into my eyes. She was biting her lip and

moaning. I looked into her eyes as I went deeper and deeper inside of her. From time to time she would close her eyes to take it all in. Her moans were no longer soft but loud. I pulled her close to me as I started to erupt in ecstasy inside of her. She softly bit my ear to try to muffle her moans, then she started sucking on my ear and kissing on my neck as I finished.

Cyan and I sat holding each other. She leaned back, looked me in my eyes, softly bit her lip and said with a soft sexy moan, *"I want to have your baby."* *"Hmmm, that's serious, baby."* I replied sort of in shock. *"Yea, I know baby, but I'm serious,"* Cyan answered back in a soft sexy voice. *"You sure boo?"* I asked. *"Yea I'm sure, baby. We've been together since we were kids and I know I want to spend the rest of my life with you. If it was up to me, we would have been married a long time ago."* *"Dang, Cyan that's deep, well what's up you want to wait until after we finish our Masters' or what?"* I asked. *"All I have to say is that I want your last name."* *"That's cool, I'll see if I can make that happen."* Cyan could tell that I was serious and wanted to marry her too. She giggled and gave me a kiss on the cheek and hugged me.

"Sincere?" Cyan said with a concerned look on her face. *"Huh?"* I answered, coming out of my daze

and realizing we were in my car. *"Baby, you were just staring at me and I was just wondering what was up?"* *"Oh, nuttin,'"* I answered back. I leaned over and gave Cyan a soft kiss on the lips, she ran her fingers and hands up my neck and grabbed my ears and kissed me back and then she wrapped her hands around my neck. I moved back and wiggled my eyebrows, bit my lip, and winked at her. Smiling at her I said, *"Girl, you need to stop because you're about to get it."* *"Well what you waiting on?"* *"Cyan is that a challenge?"* *"It can be anything you want it to be. I'm right here so what are you going to do about it? I'm all yours, so what's up?"* *"Hold that thought, we got to handle some business first."* For some reason, my heart wouldn't stop beating fast. I had big plans today. Wow. I started to think back to what Cyan said last night and I realized that Cyan and I had been together for a very long time.

We had been together since we were twelve, well you can really say our whole lives, because our families were very close, and it appeared like we were arranged to be married since the day we were born. I am only a month older than Cyan. I officially asked Cyan to be my girlfriend when we were six, but I don't think that really counts. Since we were kids, we have always been together. Everyone said that we were inseparable.

We were on our way to the mall. I kept my hands on the gearshift and Cyan's hand was on mine. She kept rubbing my hand, smiling, biting her lip, and looking at me and turning away giggling. She was looking so radiant and her presence was ethereal. All I could think about was that Cyan is my world, my heart, my everything, and she really has changed my life. She completes me. There were many times when I was frightened to be in love with her because I didn't know which way our relationship was going to go. I never wanted to lose her. Like any couple we had a few rough patches, but we made it through.

I slowly pulled into the parking lot and parked the car. I turned it off, jumped out of the driver's seat, ran to the passenger's door and let Cyan out of the car. She said, *"Thank you"* and took my hand. We slowly walked hand-in-hand towards the mall. When we got to the doors of the mall, I opened them; we walked in and headed for a jewelry shop. *"Hey Sincere,"* the store manager greeted me with a handshake. *"Hey Mr. Freeman."* *"Cyan, it is always a pleasure to see you,"* Mr. Freeman exclaimed while kissing Cyan on her hand. *"Hey Mr. Freeman, how are you?"* Cyan asked. *"Just fine and you?"* Mr. Freeman replied. *"I'm good."* *"Great, so Sincere your order is ready, did you come to pick it up?"*

Mr. Freeman asked. *"Most definitely, sir,"* I answered back. *"Okay, let me go get it then."* Mr. Freeman was in his sixties and had this business for about 40 years. Mr. Freeman was tall, dark, clean-shaven, had salt and pepper hair, and wore glasses. He had known me for my whole life; in fact, my father bought my mother's engagement ring and all of their jewelry from Mr. Freeman so of course I continued the tradition of buying jewelry from him. Cyan and I always came into the shop to get her jewelry. Mr. Freeman came back to the counter with multiple boxes. He left two boxes wrapped up in a plastic bag, which I immediately put in my pocket. Mr. Freeman and I had this preplanned. *"What was that Sincere?"* *"Oh, it's a little something for the mother."* Mr. Freeman opened the remaining boxes on the counter, which contained three 24kt. gold chains with diamond links and medallions. One said, *"I Love You,"* another said, *"Sincere"* and the other *"Cyan."* All the medallions were 24kt. gold and totally filled with diamonds. Cyan was in total shock when she saw the chains. *"Sincere, they are so beautiful."* *"Nothing compares to your beauty, Cyan."* *"So, are we pleased?"* Mr. Freeman asked the both of us. *"Oh yes I love it,"* Cyan answered back. *"Good,"* Mr. Freeman exclaimed. I thanked Mr. Freeman and shook his hand. *"Tell your parents I said hello, Sincere." "I will Mr. Freeman."* Mr. Freeman walked away to assist a customer that just walked into the store. Cyan lifted her hair and giggled while looking in the mirror as I placed the *"I Love You"* and *"Sincere"* chains around her neck. I put the *"Cyan"* chain on mine. I turned Cyan around while she was still holding her hair up; she stared at me smiling with a sexy look in her eyes. I pulled her close and kissed her and she let her hair drop. She placed her arms around my neck and gave me soft kisses. *"You are something else, Sincere,"* Cyan told me. *"Na, anything for you."* Cyan told me how she needed a couple of outfits, so I took her shopping. I mean it's not like we were hurting for money, so why not spoil my baby.

Cyan and I had recently opened a day care center/music school. Cyan also designed clothes for major retailers. My father and uncle have their own record company. My mother is the director at the new school that Cyan and I opened. Cyan's father is an entertainment lawyer and her mother is a neurosurgeon, so money was definitely not an issue for us. After all the shopping, we left the mall and walked to the car. *"Oh my gosh I feel like I am the luckiest woman in the world." "Na, I am just the luckiest man in the world." "Can the day get any better?"* Cyan asked. *"We'll just have to see,"* I answered back with a smirk. Cyan looked at me. *"What else do you have planned?" "I don't know." "Tell me Sincere, I want to know." "Na, babe it's a surprise."* I opened the door for Cyan, let her get in the car and then I put her bags in the trunk. I hopped in the car and we were back on the road. *"Baby, you hungry?"* I asked Cyan. *"Yea I guess so, what do you want to eat?" "I'll leave it up to you, it's your day." "Alright how about the High Rise?" "That sounds cool to me."* I reached over and took Cyan's hand, looked into her eyes and told her that I loved her. She smiled and told me she loved me too.

We arrived at the High Rise, which is a restaurant that overlooks the ocean. This restaurant is known as a place where a man always pops the big question. During dinner I took one of the boxes out of the bag that Mr. Freeman gave me, and I gave it to Cyan. *"Sincere, it is so beautiful."* Cyan pulled the diamond tennis bracelet out of the box. *"I thought it was for your mother." "No, I said it's a little something for the mother - the mother of my children."* Cyan's eyes filled up with tears. *"Are you serious, Sincere?" "Yea, baby you're right, I don't need to waste any more time. I want to spend my life with you too. So, after I sit down with your parents and get their blessing, yea you can definitely expect to hear the question and then you will be Mrs. Sincere Robinson in no time."* "Oh, man," I said looking at the time. *"What's up baby?"* Cyan asked. *"We got moves to make Cyan."* I motioned for the waiter, paid for the check and we got in my car and headed for the Diamond Club.

It was about 5:00 p.m. when we arrived at the Diamond Club. We had two hours until the workers would start showing up to prepare for the club's opening at 8:00 p.m. I walked Cyan into the R&B room. I walked over to the D.J. booth and set up some of our favorite songs. While dancing with Cyan I just thought of what else I had planned for the night. The last song was "our" song; it was *"For the Rest of Our Lives,"* by Jagged Edge. I checked the time as the song ended, it was 6:45 p.m. We were heading out of the club as the workers were heading in.

We hopped back in my car and headed to my house to watch the sunset. My house overlooked the beach so I could see the beautiful sunset every day. We arrived at my house, I grabbed the wireless speaker out of my car, took the blanket out of my trunk and we walked down to the beach. We sat down a few feet from where the waves washed up on the sand and I put on *"Let's Get Married"* by Jagged Edge. As we gave each other soft kisses, I reached in my pocket and pulled out the last remaining box (the other box that Mr. Freeman gave me). Cyan looked at me and asked, *"Another gift?"* *"Cyan we've been together our whole lives, we've had our ups and downs, but I truly believe this is our destiny and I just wanted to let you I know that I would be honored if you would be my wife and spend the rest of your life with me."* I opened the box, which contained a 2-carat white gold engagement ring. There was a large diamond in the middle with two smaller diamonds on each side of it. Her eyes slowly filled with tears of joy which rolled down her cheeks as I asked her to marry me. More tears fell down her face as she said yes. I gave her a kiss and laid back; she put her head on my chest as she examined her ring. As we laid on the beach watching the sunset, we fell asleep holding hands.

I woke up and saw Cyan lying on my chest. I started to smile and looked at my watch, nudged Cyan's head with mine and said, *"I thought we were watching a movie at your house tonight."* *"Oh yeah I forgot,"* Cyan said rubbing her eyes. We took everything back to my car and got in. We were on our way back to her house when we came to a stop at a red light. *"Sincere, I thought you said you had to talk to my parents before you popped the marriage question,"* Cyan said with a curious look on her face. *"What do you think I was doing when I was waiting for you to come downstairs today?"* I answered back. *"No way, are you serious?"* Cyan questioned. *"Yea, I told you I wasn't wasting any more time."*

I took her by both of her hands and told her I loved her. Cyan told me she loved me too. I was so caught up in this moment, until I heard someone scream, *"Yo, get out of the car!"* Cyan saw the love and joy in my eyes turn into concern and anger. She softly begged me to get out of the car as tears filled up in her eyes. I got out of the car and so did Cyan. As I got out the guy told me to walk around the front of the car and not to look back for any reason. I went over to Cyan and took her by the hand. Cyan told me the guy had a mask on and she could not see his face. We started walking towards the sidewalk as I pulled out my cellphone and started to call the cops, and Cyan started calling her parents. All of a sudden there was the sound of gunshots. I pulled Cyan down with me as shots rang through the air, then I sat there and watched as my brand-new BMW sped off. I got up and gave a laugh of disgust because the only thing I lost was my car and I got a minor flesh wound, so I thought. *"Stupid idiot, he doesn't even know how to use a gun."* I started snickering at the thought, but my snickering turned into pain and fear as I looked down and saw Cyan lying on the ground. I did not know what to do. She was bleeding to death, and I couldn't help her. I fell into a state of shock but quickly snapped out of it. I saw blood coming from Cyan's stomach and back. Man, a bullet entered through Cyan's stomach and exited through her back, how am I going to save her? I can't possibly stop the bleeding. I pulled Cyan close trying to keep her awake. I realized I should not have moved her. *"You're going to be fine, you're going to make it,"* I just kept repeating it over and over again. Deep down inside I knew she was slipping away. I started to scream for someone to help us, but no one was around. I picked up my cell phone and told the police I needed help; my fiancée had been shot. I knew by the time they reached me it would be too late. I couldn't stop the bleeding. As I held Cyan tight, I told her she was my angel and she told me the same. We both smiled as I pulled her close to me. I gave her a kiss and it hurt because I realized it was going to be our last. When I kissed her, it was like we were saying goodbye to each other. Our lips touched and tears started streaming down our faces. I pulled back and Cyan begged me not to let her go. *"Just hold me, Sincere. Tell my parents I love them, please."* *"You'll be fine Cyan what are you talking about?"* I said it trying to assure myself that Cyan was going to make it, but I knew otherwise. *"Sincere, you don't have to lie to me, I already know. Just tell them please,"* Cyan pleaded. *"Okay, I will." "Sincere, don't be sad, don't cry, you have made life worth living." "Cyan, please no, I can't lose you, not like this, I need you."* Cyan looked me in my eyes and said, *"I love you Sincere, you will be fine.... I promise."* I said, *"I love you Cyan,"* I took her by her hands and softly said, *"Now before GOD, I pledge my eternal love. You are my wife and I am your husband,"* and then we both said, *"Amen."*

I saw Cyan's soul leave her body. All I could do was sit there and cry; my heart was so broken that I wanted to die with her. For some reason I kept asking GOD, *"Why couldn't it have been me that died?"* but deep down in my heart a voice kept telling me it wasn't my time to go. I couldn't believe that the only woman that I ever loved and that the special lady who held the key to my heart was dead. I didn't understand how my true love that I was supposed to spend the rest of my life with was now lying lifeless in my arms. I vowed to always hold Cyan in my heart, because I knew one day we would be together, but first we had to be apart. Cyan was the queen of my heart; no one could ever take her place. The day Cyan died was the day that I lost my true love and my heart.

4 Years Later

TWO

It has been four years since I last held you, four years since I laid your body to rest, four years since I had to break the news to your parents that their one and only baby girl was dead. Who would have known that they went out on a date that night? They never got your phone call moments before you were shot. Cyan, every day I miss you more and more. Why did you have to leave? It hurts to have to live without you. Why couldn't it be me? Baby I just wish you would come back to me. I can't do this without you. I guess GOD needed his angel back home with HIM. Cyan do me a favor; ask HIM if he has room for one more?

I took a trip down to Virginia to try to clear my head. It's been four years since Cyan's death. That dreadful night plays over and over again in my head. It's so hard without Cyan sometimes. I don't even want to breathe, let alone live. If it wasn't for GOD, I don't even think I would be alive. Hopefully, this trip down to VA will do me some good. My family has been pushing me just to go. I have been doing absolutely nothing. My life feels so empty without

Cyan. I don't know if this trip is going to help, but who knows?

My cousin picked me up from the airport and immediately he could tell how depressed I was. We said our greetings and started on our way to his house. It has been a while since I've last seen my cousin. It felt good chillin' in his brand-new Lexus truck, reminiscing about old times. *"So, you want to hit up the club with the fellas tonight?"* my cousin asked. *"Na, I think I'm just gonna chill,"* I replied. *"You have to let her go man; it's been four years. I know she would be furious with you not living your life." "Yea, I know, just give me some time."*

We finally made it to Big Mama's old house. She left it to the family. My Aunt Chloe, Uncle Buba and Cousin Kaseem stayed at the house. I haven't been there ever since she passed away. I haven't even been to VA since she passed. The first thing I did was take a trip to Ebenezer Baptist Church. I looked around until I finally found it. I walked over and knelt down at the marble colored headstone. "Mary Mae Robinson, 'Big Mama'."

"Well Big Mama, I'm here, I know it's been so long. I've missed you. It's been five years. We were planning a trip to come see you, but you passed away two weeks before our surprise visit and then a year later Cyan was killed. I guess GOD needed y'all to

come home to do some work in heaven. Big Mama, I miss her so much. Give her a hug and kiss for me and tell her that I love her and one more thing...Big Mama I love you." I got up and walked back to Big Mama's house.

On my way back to Big Mama's house, I ran into Jaheim, Khalil, Roscoe and Ray, my old VA buddies. Jaheim and Khalil were brothers, Ray and Roscoe were brothers and they also happened to be Jaheim and Khalil's cousins. Whenever I came down to VA, I hung out with them. It's been five years since I've seen them last. *"Look who finally decided to grace us with his presence." "Whatever Khalil, how have y'all been?"* was my reply to Khalil's remark. *"Everything's the same,"* said Jaheim. *"Where are you heading to?"* asked Roscoe. *"Back to Big Mama's house,"* I replied. *"We're heading to New York tomorrow,"* Ray exclaimed. *"Yea your neck of the woods Sin." "Oh word? Y'all have fun,"* was my reply. *"Later,"* was said by all simultaneously. We went our separate ways; nothing had changed with any of us, it's like we picked up right where we left off.

I missed sitting on the porch looking up at the stars. It's been so long. I remember when Big Mama used to sit me on her lap and tell me stories about her childhood, about my father's childhood and all the stories her mother and grandmother told her. I used to fall asleep in her arms and she would tuck me in. Oh, how I missed those summers.

Jaheim and Khalil came by the next day and we walked to their house. I needed to get some fresh air. Their house was about a 10-minute walk from Big Mama's house. I needed that walk; it was soothing. It also gave me a chance to catch up on what was going on in my buddies' lives. When we arrived at their house, I talked to their parents for a little while and then we went to go grab a bite to eat at the Waffle House. After spending a couple of hours together we went back to their house. From there I headed to Big Mama's house. As I was leaving, Khalil called to me, *"Ay Sin did you say hey to Aunt Catherine yet?" "No not yet, but I will,"* I answered back. My buddies' Aunt Catherine lived across the street from Big Mama's house. *"Oh yeah,"* Khalil added, *"Our little cousin Savannah is coming to live with Aunt Catherine." "Really?" "Yea, she used to live in New York and started her own fashion magazine company. She moved to North Carolina to expand her company and now she is coming to start another branch of the magazine here in Virginia."*

As I walked back to Big Mama's house, I saw Khalil and Jaheim's Aunt Cat (that's what I always called her), struggling to bring bags into her house. I immediately went across the street to give her a hand. *"Thank you Sincere,"* Aunt Cat said with a smile. *"You're welcome Aunt Cat."* *"Sincere?"* Aunt Cat said, doing a double take. *"Baby, how are you, when did you get into town?"* *"I am hanging in there, Aunt Cat. I actually just got here yesterday,"* I replied. *"Baby I am so sorry about Cyan, it's such a shame,"* she said, putting her hand on my shoulder. I tried not to cry as I said, *"it's alright Aunt Cat."* After I was done helping Aunt Cat I went and sat on the swinging chair on Big Mama's porch. I was awakened by a beautiful 5'5", medium brown complexion, bluish – green eyed, collar-length haired young woman. When I awoke, she smiled and said, *"Well, nice of you to wake up, I thought I would be here all night."* She started giggling and I chuckled. *"Hi, I'm Sincere, can I help you with something?"* I sat up, staring at the young lady; her eyes…. I had to look away. She said with a smile, *"I'm Savannah, it's nice to meet you. My cousins told me about you; you are the one from New York with the daycare center/music school."* *"Yea,"* I answered. *"My Aunt wanted me to give you this cake she made for you for helping her out."* Savannah handed me the covered cake plate. *"Well, I gotta run I'll talk to you later,"* Savannah said while looking at her watch.

THREE

"Tell my parents that I miss them," were my words to my Aunt Chloe, Uncle Buba, and Kaseem as they went to go visit my parents and my family in New York. This was something that they used to do every summer. Uncle Buba visited frequently throughout the year since he ran the record label with my father. *"We will,"* said my Aunt Chloe and Uncle Buba. *"Ay, yo take care of my baby,"* my cousin Kaseem said referring to his brand-new Lexus SUV. Just as they pulled away, Savannah walked over to ask me if I had enjoyed the cake that her aunt made for me for helping her out yesterday. *"Of course I enjoyed it,"* I replied. *"So, you want to hang out, catch a movie, or a bite to eat?"* Savannah asked. *"Na, not really,"* was my reply. Even though Savannah was looking really fine, I just couldn't do it. I thought to myself, she'll never be Cyan so why should I even bother befriending a woman? *"Okay...why are you trying to brush me off, it's not a date?"* Savannah asked curiously. *"Number one I don't even know you like you that, number two I don't have female friends and I'm not looking for*

any," I answered back. *"Okay, first you hang out with someone in order to get to know them and second you won't even try to get to know me? What is wrong with you? What is your deal?"* replied Savannah. *"Nothing…look I'm sorry…just let it go, I don't feel like talking about it."* At that I walked into the house. I watched as Savannah walked back to her Aunt's house. I kept thinking to myself I don't want to hurt her. I don't want the same thing that happened with Cyan to happen with Savannah too. My heart is too fragile. I had everything I ever wanted and needed taken away from me. My heart, my soul, everything ripped out of me and all I could do was watch helplessly. *"Savannah I'm sorry, this is the best thing for the both of us,"* I whispered softly to myself.

The next day Khalil and Jaheim were on their way to my house and while still a few yards away, Khalil saw me sitting in the swing on the porch and hollered, *"What up Sin?"* *"What's the deal fam?"* I hollered back. *"Did you meet Savannah yet?"* asked Jaheim. *"Yeah I met her yesterday,"* I answered back. *"Aunt Catherine told our mom how you helped her out yesterday,"* Khalil said. *"Yea it was no big deal man,"* I replied. *"What up punks?"* Savannah yelled as she was walking across the street. *"Is that how you talk to your older cousins, squirt?"* Jaheim yelled back. Savannah reached us. *"You know what? I just wish the whole family was here. I miss Ray and Roscoe,"* Savannah said sadly, *"Yea we do too,"* replied Jaheim and Khalil. *"Hey why don't we go to the store and get something to eat?"* Savannah asked. I declined but Jaheim and Khalil went with Savannah.

"What's up with Sincere fellas? I mean, what's his deal?" Savannah asked. *"Well he hasn't been the same since his fiancée was murdered four years ago,"* Khalil replied. *"Yea murdered right in front of his face and then dude jacked Sincere for his brand-new Beamer too,"* Jaheim added. *"Cyan died in his arms as he watched helplessly,"* stated Khalil. *"Don't take it personal little cuz, Sincere hasn't let any female close to his heart since Cyan was killed and besides, you also have…her eyes,"* Jaheim said shaking his head. Savannah said, *"He must be real hurt and sad, wait…what do you mean her eyes?"* Savannah finally realized what was said. *"Same eye color,"* Jaheim replied and then nodded his head while he was looking at Khalil. *"Yea,"* Jaheim and Khalil replied sadly.

I was sitting on the porch swing again when Savannah approached me and asked, *"Sincere, what happened four years ago?"* *"Nothing, what are you talking about?"* I asked back, real hurt. I tried to shrug it off like it was nothing, but I could feel it tearing me apart from the inside out. *"You know… to Cyan,"* Savannah replied. *"Who told you about Cyan?"* I asked with tears in my eyes. *"I don't want to talk about it,"* I added. *"Why?"* Savannah asked. *"Because, I just don't want to, now can you please leave me alone?"* I stated angry, hurt, and upset all at the same time. At that I went inside and slammed the door behind me. I turned around and banged on the door as the tears started to burn my face. I was in pain and agony; I didn't know what to do. It's like I couldn't catch my breath. I had to sit down with my back against the door and to calm myself down. After finally catching a hold of myself, I went back outside and sat on the swinging chair.

"…Cyan no don't leave me, please wake up, I need you, Cyan I love you. Please don't do this to me…I can't do this without you!" I woke up sweating and found myself being patted on the head with a cool washrag. It felt so good. I laid back down and let the tears roll out of my eyes and down my face. I was so mixed up in my dream world that I was surprised when I heard someone softly crying over me. I looked up - it was Savannah. *"What are you doing here?"* I asked softly. *"I was coming over to apologize for bringing the whole Cyan issue up. You must have dozed off and I saw you sweating real bad. I*

thought you had a fever, so I ran and got a bowl of cool water and a wash rag. I laid your head on my lap and began to pat your head down. That's when you started talking in your sleep. I felt so bad for you, it's like you were reliving Cyan's death all over again. I started crying because I had to sit helplessly and watch and let you relive it. I wanted to wake you up, but it's like my whole body just froze and I couldn't move. There was nothing I could do, and I felt so bad about it." "It's not your fault Savannah," I replied. *"It's no one's fault,"* I added. Savannah sat rubbing my head and we both dozed off. I woke up out of nowhere and looked at my watch. It was 2:45 A.M. I woke Savannah up and walked her over to her aunt's house. *"Thank you for staying with me, because you didn't have to,"* I said. *"Anytime, it's not a problem,"* Savannah answered back. I kissed her on her cheek and went back home.

I was awakened the next morning by a warm body up underneath me. I looked down to see Savannah fast asleep. *"Savannah what are you doing here?"* I asked half asleep. *"I came by to check on you and your door was unlocked. I came in, locked it, and came upstairs. I found you asleep and didn't want to wake you, so I just got in the bed with you. I hope you don't mind,"* Savannah replied. *"Look I don't have anything against you but I'm about to go on the floor, because I hardly know you and I can't just be in the bed with you like that." "That's understandable and I respect you for that Sincere,"* Savannah replied. *"So, tell me what happened to Cyan, Sincere."* Savannah asked. *"I mean, if you are up to it,"* Savannah added. I let out a big sigh and started explaining. *"Cyan and I started dating when we were like twelve, but we have been together our whole lives because we grew up together. We were together all through junior high and high school. We graduated and went on to college. We both graduated a year early from Hofstra University. I have a Bachelor's in Music Education and Cyan had a Bachelor's in Early Childhood Education. We were chilling out for the summer about to go back for our Masters. We had opened the school up and no one could believe that we accomplished so much by the age of 21. I wanted to marry Cyan before the school year started, but I just didn't have the nerve to ask. She visited her aunt, uncle, and cousins in North Carolina for like a month, which left us missing each other like crazy. When she got home, we met at my brother Quinton and her cousin Esco's club, the Diamond Club. I remember it like it was yesterday. My boys and Cyan's girls had met up and were kickin' it while I was scoping the room for Cyan. Esco came up to me and told me that Cyan was sitting at a booth. Me and Cyan locked eyes and that was that. I walked up to the ta-ble cool and calm; I was trying to hold back my excitement, because I hadn't seen her in a minute. Just seeing her made my heart rush."* I stopped for a moment and just smiled, reflecting on Cyan made me feel so good, but it hurt so bad at the same time. *"An-yway, the next day I asked her parents for their blessing because I wanted to ask Cyan to marry me. They gladly gave their blessing. I had the whole day planned. I took Cyan to the mall and gave her a dia-mond "I Love You" and "Sincere" name plate and I had a diamond "Cyan" name plate for myself that I had specially ordered. I took Cyan out to eat at the High Rise for dinner and gave her a diamond tennis bracelet. I then took her out to the Diamond Club where it was just us. I had all of our favorite songs playing. Our "last" dance together was to "For the Rest of Our Lives" by Jagged Edge. I took her to my house after the club so that we could watch the sunset as we sat on the beach. We laid down on a blanket and just looked at the sky as the sun finished setting while we talked. That's when I proposed and with tears in her eyes she said yes. We fell asleep feeling like the happiest and luckiest couple in the world. We woke up and got in the car so we could go to her house."* I tried to fight the tears that were starting to fill my eyes. *"We were driving and so into each other, that when we came to a stop light, we didn't see the guy rolling up on the car. He told us to get out of the car, which we did after Cyan pleaded with her eyes for me to get out. I was walking Cyan to the sidewalk while I tried to contact the cops and Cyan tried to contact her parents to let them know what happened. I heard gunshots and my car screeched off. I got up and checked myself and laughed because I saw that I only had a flesh wound, but when I turned around, I saw Cyan lying on the ground bleeding to death."*

At that time, the tears started pouring out of my eyes and the lumps started building in my throat. *"Savannah there was nothing I could do, I felt like it was all my fault. I wasn't mad about my car; I pleaded to GOD, please don't take my baby away from me, LORD. I talked to Cyan and told her how much I loved her and how much I needed her. Cyan with her beautiful bluish green eyes told me to be strong and she promised me that I would be fine. We both said I love you and then I watched her spirit leave her and I saw her take my heart, soul, and everything that I was with her. After Cyan died, I didn't go back to school; I fell into a very deep depression. Savannah how could I be strong when I needed her? I miss her so much, I still can feel her touch, her smell, and everything about her is in my heart. Some-times I can't sleep at night because of nightmares. Some days my heart hurts and I can't breathe. My life is just a mess sometimes, I can't control it, and I just can't get a hold of anything. Sometimes I don't feel like living, I feel like giving up on everything."* By now the tears were burning as they continuously streamed down my face. *"Savannah, I couldn't stop I.... why couldn't I have kept Cyan alive? Why couldn't it be me who took the bullet? It wasn't fair; it wasn't supposed to happen like that. We were supposed to die old and happy together after having a large family. Cyan died the night I proposed to her."* Shaking and crying at the same time I realized that I had lost it. With tears streaming out of her eyes, Savannah came over to me, hugged me and told me everything would be okay. All I could do was continuously repeat, *"it's not fair."*

I woke up to find myself in Savannah's arms; we were both sitting on the floor against the wall. I asked Savannah, *"Why are you still here?"* *"It's okay; you were having a rough time and I didn't feel comfortable leaving you here by yourself."* Savannah replied. *"Well I can't be mad at that, thank you for being here Savannah."*

Over time Savannah and I became good friends. A year had passed, and Savannah's parents were about to move down to VA, so Aunt Cat went to visit with them to help them start moving and taking care of the final paperwork for the move. Aunt Cat was a Real Estate Agent and she was handling the closing of Savannah's parent's house. Savannah's father was finishing up his 35th year with the Sheriff's Department. Instead of coming back like they normally do at the end of the summer, Aunt Chloe, Uncle Buba and Cousin Kaseem continued to stay at my house in New York. Aunt Chloe started working with my mother at my school; Kaseem was third in charge at the record company helping my father and Uncle Buba. Savannah didn't really want to stay in her Aunt's house by herself, so I offered to let her stay with me in Big Mama's house. We were cool and all, so I really didn't see a problem.

I cooked Savannah dinner that night. We sat down and the first words I said after grace were, *"I'm sorry for the way that I treated you Savannah; it was rough coming into contact with another woman after losing the only woman I ever loved." "It's okay, I understand why you acted the way you did. If I was in the same situation, I would have probably acted the same way,"* Savannah replied. *"Savannah what was your life like before you came to Virginia?"* I asked. *"It was okay; great family life, great career, but relationship-wise I was never treated right. I was not loved like I truly deserved to be loved" "What, a smart, beautiful, and talented woman like you? No way, I would have thought that men would be beating down your door asking you to marry them." "Please, not even close, Sincere." "I'm really sorry to hear that, don't let that get you down Savannah,"* I replied. *"Life goes on, things can only get better,"* I added. *"Yea, you're right Sincere, but tell me something why can't you follow your own advice?"* Savannah asked. *"I don't know. I've been great at giving advice, but I can never seem to follow my own,"* I answered with a chuckle. *"Well, you need to learn,"* Savannah answered back with a smirk on her face.

As time went by, Savannah was getting closer to my heart each day. I was scared but I learned it was time to stop pushing her away. I decided to let her help me cook. She was going to help me cook my "famous" chicken and rice dinner. It was famous to me at least. Savannah rang the doorbell after returning from the store with the groceries and another bag, which she claimed to be a surprise for me. She came in and the bag that was "my surprise," she placed in my room.

Savannah cut the carrots, red peppers, and onions. *"I'm done,"* she said as I finished boiling the rice. I started cooking the chicken and after that was done, we started mixing everything together. I set the dinner out on the table and Savannah went upstairs to my room and locked the door. When she was done, she called me to the stairs as she slowly started walking down. Savannah had on a long black dress that made her look so sexy it left me speechless. Her beauty was more than words could explain. She looked like an angel even though she was dressed in black. She finally reached the bottom of the steps and just waiting for her had my heart pounding. She walked up to me and I hugged her. Her warm body up against me felt so good, I didn't even realize I was holding her for a minute. When I finally realized it, I backed up, but she grabbed me tighter and said, *"Don't fight it, because I'm not."* Out of nowhere I hugged her tighter and said, *"I love you."* We both backed up and looked into each other's eyes; I was in complete shock. I immediately said, *"I'm sorry." "No don't be sorry, if that's how you feel then baby, don't fight it,"* Savannah replied, grabbing my hands and putting them around her. Savannah came closer and I gently kissed her. I became lost in her love; it was like I could feel all her love and passion in her kiss. After we caught a hold of ourselves, we sat down to eat.

We sat staring and smiling at each other as the candlelight blazed. After dinner was finished, I moved next to her and took her by the hand. We talked and laughed about our first impressions of each other, stories about our families, and our lives. After our conversation Savannah started to get up and get the dishes. I told her don't worry about it because I would do them, and she insisted, but I was not letting her wash dishes in that pretty dress. She sat on the couch and I sat with her after I finished. I took her hand and motioned for her to come closer; I placed her in between my legs with her back facing me. I told her that I wanted to thank her for her help, so I started massaging her back. I started massaging her neck and slowly moved aside the shoulder straps of her dress so I could fully massage her shoulder. All I kept thinking to myself is how Savannah's soft body felt so good. Her body looked tempting enough to eat. I had the urge to just kiss all over her, but I kept telling myself, I'm a gentleman and that's not my style. Savannah isn't technically my lady and I can't make moves on her like that.

It was like I couldn't help myself. I totally went against my rules when I started kissing her neck and started nibbling on her ear very softly. Savannah started moaning and she grabbed my head gently as I started rubbing her back and then I stopped. Savannah asked, *"Why did you stop?"* I couldn't believe how heated she was. I told her, *"I can't let it happen like this, Savannah. I want to do this right. I want you to be my woman, not just be another woman in my life.*" She said, "*Okay.*" Savannah went upstairs and changed into a pair of sweats, a cut off t-shirt and she wrapped her hair up in a scarf. She came over to me and put her head on my lap. I started rubbing her head and back. "*You know, I really respect you for what you did, Sincere. You know stopping so it wouldn't go any further.*" "*Thanks Savannah,*" I replied. "*It felt so right, but I know I couldn't let it happen like that, I didn't want you to be one of my friends with special privileges or benefits. I respect you and you need to be treated like the queen that you are, that's why I would want you to be my lady before we start getting intimate.*" "*Tell me something Sincere?*" "*Yea Savannah?*" "*Did you really want me?*" "*Oh yeah, like you wouldn't believe,*" I replied in a very deep tone. At that we both started laughing. Savannah turned over, pulled me close to her, kissed me, and whispered, "*I love you.*" As she pulled away, I looked into her eyes and had a brief flash of Cyan during our last kiss. I snapped out of it really quick. "*Is something wrong Sincere?*" Savannah asked with a look of concern. I smiled and said, "*Na, everything is just fine.*" Savannah laid back, smiled at me, and went to sleep. I rubbed her head and her stomach until I dozed off.

I woke up the next morning, gave Savannah a kiss on the forehead and gently eased out from under her so I would not wake her up. I went into the kitchen. I wanted to surprise her by making her breakfast. I walked back into the living room where we fell asleep, just to get another glimpse of her as she slept. I kept asking myself, did last night really happen? Was it real? After catching hold of reality, I headed back into the kitchen. What am I doing? I must be crazy, I can't do that to Savannah, and I can't do that to Cyan. I feel so wrong.

I cooked some eggs, pancakes, bacon, home fries and poured some orange juice. I put everything on the table next to Savannah and woke her up with another kiss on the forehead. She smiled, looked around, and then said, *"All of this for me?"* I said *"Yea."* Looking at Savannah, I realized I was falling in love with her. This woman has moved so close to my heart, I don't know what I would do without her. I refused to let her take Cyan's place in my heart though.

"...Cyan I'm sorry, I miss you so much. I don't know what to do. I know I've been holding on to you for five years, and I love you more than anything, no woman can ever compare to you. I need to stop whatever is going on with Savannah before it goes too far, before anything happens between us."

"Savannah this can't be, I'm just not ready for a relationship and we should just be friends. No, no, no that's all wrong, I can't approach her like that," I kept repeating my thoughts aloud to hear if they sounded right. Just then Savannah walked up to me while my head was down. I looked up, gave her a hug, and she started kissing me. Her warm soft lips pressed up against mine sent a rush through my body. *"Savannah wait,"* I said backing up. *"No, stop fighting me,"* Savannah replied. *"Let's settle this right now. Just tell me you don't love me, and I'll leave you alone, Sincere." "Savannah, I Can't."* I pulled her close to me and kissed her.

That night Savannah stayed with me and we slept in the same bed. Nothing happened, we just stayed up all night talking and laughing…well that's all I thought we were going to do. I woke up in the middle of the night to Savannah wrapping her legs around me while she rubbed my chest with her soft delicate hands. I kept thinking to myself, I have to stop this, but it feels so good. She started to slowly move up on top of me, then I slowly took her hands, gave her a kiss and said, *"Let's not take it further than it's supposed to go." "You know Sincere, so far you're passing all of my tests; you're not like any of the other guys who would just love to get in between a woman's legs." "Na, I'm nothing like that. Intimacy is a very sacred thing that should be shared between two people that are in love with each other. I mean really in love, like that "dangerously in love" kind of love. The kind of love where you never want to be without each other, like that "you've got it bad" kind of love." "I totally agree Sincere. So how much in love are you with me?" "I'm definitely in love; I just want to wait to make love to you, because I want it to be a surprise and special. I don't want it to be just out of horniness. Besides you're not ready for me to turn you out,"* I said with a grin. *"Ooooo, you're so nasty."* At that Savannah and I started giggling. We fell asleep to me rubbing her head and back. Her body felt so good. She was laying on my chest, so it was like she fell asleep to my heartbeat. I'm not gonna lie, I wanted her more than anything. Especially since it's been 5 years since I got any kind of affection from a woman. I just wanted it to be really special.

Earlier during the day, Savannah and I agreed that we would have a romantic evening and that I would cook for her. I spent most of the day shopping to make sure tonight would be a great night. Savannah walked through the door in this really long, dark blue dress. The dress had two long slits up the sides. Whenever she took a step it would expose a little bit of her sexy legs. She walked in knowing that she was turning me on. I took her jacket off, hung it up and walked back to her. I held her from behind and kissed her on her neck and then started rubbing her on her arms. She turned around and wrapped her arms around my neck and then she pulled my head to her and started kissing me. After we finished kissing, I told her to save some for later. I pulled her chair out and she sat down. I made her filet mignon with asparagus tips dipped in creamed spinach. After dinner she told me how delicious it was. We sat talking for a couple more hours. *"Sincere, it's getting late and I am a little tired. I hate to end the evening so early with you because I enjoy spending time with you." "You sure you just don't want to stay the night?" "Not tonight Sincere, maybe tomorrow."* I walked Savannah across the street and gave her a kiss goodnight. I headed back to Big Mama's house, went upstairs and jumped in bed.

"No, you can't go. Please don't leave." I woke up in a cold sweat. I reached over, picked up the phone and dialed Savannah's number. *"Hello,"* Savannah answered half asleep. *"Baby, come over,"* I replied. *"What? Sincere, stop playing." "Na, baby I'm serious, I need to see you,"* I replied with a serious tone. *"Sincere, are you alright, is everything okay?"* Savannah asked, concerned. Before I could answer, Savannah said, *"Give me a minute, I'll be*

right there." I got up, threw on the black silk pajama shirt that went with the black silk pajama pants I was wearing, put rose petals on my bed and then lead a trail from my bed to the front door. Savannah came over in a long jacket with a red ribbon holding her hair in place. *"What's all of this?"* she asked, looking at all the rose petals. I pulled her close to me and held her. *"Baby are you alright, you had me worried?"* I slipped her jacket off. She was wearing these sexy red silk panties and a red silk bra with a medium length red silk robe. *"I just needed to see you; I'm sorry that I worried you,"* I said. I stopped hugging her and took her by the hand. I started to walk her up to my bedroom. Savannah told me that she loves rose petals because she thinks they are so romantic. We got to my room and she was surprised to see the candle lights with the blue lava lamp flowing.

"Did you plan this, Sincere?" Savannah asked in this real soft, but playful voice. *"No, I got up and my bedroom was like this,"* I replied with a small sly chuckle. *"You are a horrible liar! Oh my gosh, you are so bad,"* Savannah said giggling. In a small whisper I told Savannah to bring her sexy body over to me. Savannah walked over and hugged me; her body pressed up against mine felt so good. My heart started pounding. I tried to keep my composure, but

I couldn't keep it long. I softly whispered in Savannah's ear. *"Savannah, I know we are both scared, but I have developed indescribable feelings for you, and I want to know if you would do me the honor of being my lady?"* Savannah answered, *"I would love to."* I found myself kissing Savannah and rubbing her body. I started rubbing and caressing her butt. I felt Savannah start to breathe harder and she started softly moaning and putting pressure on my head and neck with her hands and nails. We were both hot. I can't believe this is happening. Just as things were getting really heated, Savannah stopped me. *"Baby, hold that thought."* Savannah said and walked into the bathroom. I pulled back the covers on my bed. Savannah returned. I pulled her close by her silk red belt. *"You really wear this to sleep?"* I asked curiously. *"No, I thought something was wrong and came over here to make you feel better,"* Savannah replied. *"Oh,"* is the only thing I could say. I started kissing her and rubbing her again and realized something was different. I moved my hands down to her waist and slipped my hands under her robe. I moved my hands up her leg all the way up to her butt. Savannah was completely naked under her robe. I moved her body even closer to me, so close that you couldn't tell where she began and I ended. We looked like a black and red yin and yang sign. I took my hands and put them through the opening of Savannah's robe and started rubbing her back. Savannah moved her hands down and slipped my shirt off. She then started to unfasten the string to my pants. She then laced her hands under my arms and started rubbing her nails up and down my back. I started kissing her neck and moved down to the middle of her chest as I opened her robe up more and more. I softly lifted her up and carried her over to my bed. I slowly laid her on the bed and started kissing her beautiful breasts. She grabbed my head and started pushing my face closer and closer putting her breasts deeper into my face and mouth. That started turning me on more than she could even imagine. I pulled the covers over us as I continued to kiss, lick, and gently suck her nipples. She gently dug her nails into my back and started scratching it. I lifted my head and kissed her on the cheek.

I reached under her, and as she arched her back, she wrapped her arms and legs around me. I lifted her up and moved her so that she was on top of me. As she was holding me, we sat up. I pulled her close to me and felt her heart beating against mine. Her breasts against my chest felt so erotic. Savannah pushed me back on the bed, started kissing my chest, and started softly biting my nipples. I pulled her up and she started kissing me on my neck, as we sat up again. I put my hands under her thigh and slowly lifted her in the air. She wrapped her legs around me as we started kissing. She started rubbing her hands up and down my back, and the rubbing eventually turned into a gentle scratching. I lifted her up a little as we both took my pants off and slipped off her robe. I took her by her arms and looked her in her beautiful eyes and asked, *"Are you sure you want this, and you want it to go further?"* *"Yes, Sincere,"* she replied in a horny whisper. I slipped on a condom as she softly bit my lip. I lifted her thighs and placed her down. I felt like I was entering the softest place on earth. She gave out a moan that let me know that she had been waiting for this moment for a long time. Entering Savannah's soft, warm, moist, most intimate place gave me shivers all over. She pulled me close to her body as she whispered, *"I love you."* I slowly rolled us over and laid her on the bed as I gave her soft gentle strokes. She started to moan and rubbed her legs up and down my body. Although still gentle, the strokes started to become faster and Savannah started breathing harder and her moans started to sound like soft cries, cries that sounded like a cry for more. Her nails dug deeper and deeper into my back. At that moment I knew her body was getting extreme pleasure. I started kissing her on her neck. I felt Savannah start to shiver, her legs were now pulled closer to her body and she started moaning even louder as she started to have an orgasm. I felt her body tense up and felt her get even wetter. Savannah felt so good that my heart was beating harder and I felt my stomach tighten. I kissed Savannah as I felt my body starting to melt into her. I saw and felt Savannah's tears as I started to erupt inside of her. At that moment Savannah gave out extreme loud moans, and her legs were fully contracted to her body. Her nails dug so hard into my back that it hurt and felt so good at the same time. When we were done, I kissed Savannah and told her I loved her, she said it back, and then we fell asleep holding each other. Our naked bodies up against each other was a feeling that I would never forget.

Savannah woke up before me, slipped her robe on and went downstairs to fix me breakfast. I reached over and started twisting a rose petal with my fingers. I started smiling and replayed what took place between Savannah and I in my head. Savannah brought me up some waffles with home fries and orange juice. I told her to come and eat with me as she set the tray down next to me. We shared the breakfast. Savannah moved the tray into a corner on the floor. She then laid down while I started talking to her. I pulled her robe back over her shoulder exposing her back. I climbed on top of her and started to massage her back. I grabbed the bottle of syrup and poured a little on her. I kissed it off which really turned her on. I said *"Aw, now you're sticky so I guess we have to go get in the shower,"* I gave her a slick grin and moved my eyebrows up and down. *"You are so bad baby,"* Savannah replied. I got off of her; she got up and threw me my robe. I went into the bathroom and had a new idea. I filled the Jacuzzi up instead of running the shower. Savannah came in and let me take her robe off as she entered the water. I took my robe off as I entered the water and sat down. Savannah came over to me and sat up against me as I wrapped my arms around her, then I got a washcloth and started washing her back. *"Did you enjoy last night, ma?"* I asked. Savannah said with a moan, *"Yea, baby I really liked it, in fact I want more. Sincere, what took you so long? I know you wanted to make love to me for a really long time, so why did you wait?"* *"I did not want to be intimate with you if we're not in a committed relationship. I just couldn't do that to you. What made you start crying Savannah?"* *"I don't know…it felt so good, so right, it was so beautiful. I really wanted it, the way we were both sweating and giving each other our all, what else was there to do?"* *"I feel ya, I was just curious."* I started rubbing Savannah's arm and started kissing her on her neck. She said, *"You better stop, that's what got you in trouble last night."* At that we both started laughing. *"What happened last night baby?"* Savannah asked. *"I don't know, I guess we were both heated,"* was my reply. *"We had to be because you had me in the air."* At that moment Savannah licked her lips in a sexual way and gave a sexy giggle. *"I want to move in with you, Sincere." "Savannah we literally just started dating and now you are talking about marriage type of moves." "So, let's get married then." "We need more time, we don't even know each other like that, not enough to get married at least." "Do you want to marry me?" "Yea, I guess, but not yet." "You guess?" "Yea I do." "So, what's the problem? Do you love me?"* Savannah asked before I could answer the first question. *"Yea, I love you." "So, what is it? I'm good enough to sleep with but not good enough to marry?" "Come on ma you know it's nothing like that." "So, what's it like Sincere?"* Savannah's eyes started to fill up with tears. *"You know, all you men are just the same, you want to sleep with a woman so bad and then you don't want to commit."* I started thinking to myself, what is going on? What did I do wrong? What happened between last night and now? *"Savannah why are you acting like this?"* I asked very hurt. *"Forget it, I'm out."* At that Savannah got out of the water, dried herself off, put back on her bra, panties, robe, coat, and left. I got out of the Jacuzzi, dried off and just sat on the bed in disbelief. I went and sat in the rocking chair that Big Mama use to rock in. I couldn't grasp the fact that things just went wrong between me and Savannah. I don't get it. I tried calling Savannah, but she wouldn't answer the phone. I went over and rang the doorbell, but she wouldn't answer the door. Savannah was acting really weird. I started reflecting on what happened in the past year to try to figure out what led us to this exact moment. I seriously needed an answer so let's see… I stayed longer than I was supposed to and now I live in VA. My aunt, uncle, and cousin decided to move to New York to be with my family (Even though I think this was my family's plan all along). Ray and Roscoe had come back home from visiting New York. So pretty much nothing drastic had happened so, what could the issue be?

Ray and Roscoe came by my house and Jaheim and Khalil were on their way over. *"What's bugging Savannah y'all?"* I asked them very curiously. *"Well, a lot of things,"* replied Roscoe. *"She misses her parents for one,"* added Ray. *"She's madly in love with you,"* said Jaheim while walking up behind me. *"You've given her everything she wants in a relationship,"* Khalil said summing everything up. *"Ray and Roscoe, what took you guys so long to come back down, you were supposed to only be gone for the summer?" "Our parents fell in love with New York and decided to stay longer,"* Ray answered. *"When did Kaseem come get the Lexus?"* Roscoe asked curiously. *"Oh, when they decided to move to NY for good,"* I replied. *"Wait they left Big Mama's house to you?"* questioned Khalil. *"Yea, man. They felt it would be best if I stayed down here, you know for a change?"* I answered back. *"Where's Aunt Catherine? She's been gone for a while,"* I asked. *"Well, she went to New York and met up with us, but then she went to Alabama to go be with our grand-mother." "Well, actually I think they'll be here this weekend." "Ja, how are y'all related to Savannah?" "Well Roscoe and Ray's mom, Savannah's father, and me and Khalil's mom are siblings." "Oh, okay and your Aunt Catherine would make the third girl?" "Yea and actually she is the oldest." "Three girls and one boy, that's a nice outcome,"* I added to Jaheim's comment. *"Sincere, can I talk to you?"* I heard Savannah say over my shoulder. I played it off like I was still talking to the fellas. *"Sincere, don't do this to me."* I turned around and looked at Savannah standing with tears starting to form in her eyes. *"Oh, look at who decides to grace us with their presence fellas."* Everyone said what's up to Savannah except for me. *"Long time no see,"* Savannah said to Roscoe and Ray. *"What's up fellas?"* Savannah said to Jaheim and Khalil. *'We'll leave y'all two alone,"* Jaheim said as him and Khalil walked towards their house. *"Later,"* said Ray as him and Roscoe went to try to catch up with Jaheim and Khalil. Khalil turned around and while walking backwards said *"Sincere, remember what I said."* Khalil turned back around and continued to walk with the others.

Well that just left me and Savannah staring in each other's face. Her face had a look of pain; I had a look of disgust. *"What do you want?"* I asked very mean. *"You Sincere, all I want is you,"* Savannah answered back. *"You have a hard way of showing it,"* I shot back. *"I was scared, baby." "Of what ma?" "I don't want to lose you." "What are you talking about?" "You said you are not ready to marry me, and I know you have to eventually go home to NY, so if you left it would be over between us and we would never be together again." "Savannah, I would have never asked you to be with me if I was going to leave." "Really?"* asked Savannah. *"Yes really. Anyway, my family decided to let me have Big Mama's house because they felt the best thing for me to do is to stay here and start a new life." "Are you playing with me, Sincere?" "No, I'm serious."* At that Savannah walked up to me and grabbed my hands and kissed them; *"I am so sorry for the way I've been acting; can you ever find it in your heart to forgive me?"* I slowly took my hands out of hers, backed up, and said, *"No." "What?"* [Savannah looked at me so hurt and a couple of tears rolled down her cheek. I turned around and walked in the house. I closed the door and watched through the window at Savannah slowly walking over to the chair, where she sat and started crying…. Na, let me stop playing it really didn't happen like that. Do you really think I'm that mean? Okay, where was I? OH yeah…] At that Savannah walked up to me and grabbed my hands and kissed them; *"I am so sorry for the way I've been acting; can you ever find it in your heart to forgive me?"* I slowly took my hands out of hers and opened my arms. *"Come here, of course I forgive you."* Savannah walked into my arms with tears falling from her eyes and we held each other as the tears started rolling down my cheek. I was so happy to have Savannah in my arms. *"I don't want to fight anymore baby,"* Savannah said. *"I don't want to either."*

The weekend finally got here, and Savannah's grandmother came to visit them. She told them how she missed her family and wanted everyone to move to Alabama. She said things have not been the same in Virginia since her best friend had passed away six years ago. *"I miss her too, Mama Jo."* *"Oh, Sincere, my little baby how have you been? I heard about your fiancée Cyan and I was devastated. First my heart broke for you when Mary passed. My heart broke even more to find out that Cyan was taken from you the following year. Sincere, I know only GOD brought you through that." "Mama Jo, GOD's been real good to me, because with so many losses, I've also gained." "Bless your heart child; I hear my granddaughter is crazy about you." "Yes ma'am, and I'm crazy about her too." "Oh, that's so sweet, y'all gonna get married and have lots of babies, oh it's so beautiful." "I'm hoping we will get married, but I want to talk to her father about that first." "Such a gentleman, I am sure your parents are proud of you." "I hope they are, Mama Jo." "My son and daughter-in-law are so excited to meet you, they're coming down next weekend, but the rest of us will be gone."*

The summer was almost over and this time instead of going to New York, my friends were moving to Alabama. Aunt Cat went with them to get everyone settled in, as she was handling all the closings. Savannah and I were the only ones left in VA. Her parents would be down in a couple of days. Savannah stayed with me.

The night before Savannah's parents came down to VA, I woke up surrounded by candles blazing and saw Savannah standing at the end of my bed in a long see-through black night gown. She was wearing a black thong under it. There were black stripes on the gown; one of the stripes covered half of Savannah's breast. She lifted the bottom of the night gown up to her knees and she started crawling on me as if she were a lioness about to give the deathblow to her prey. She kissed me, turned me over, then got up for a second; what she did, I don't know but before I could figure it out, she was on my back. She started massaging my back and started kissing me on my neck. That's when I figured out what she had done. I felt her dripping on my lower back; it actually felt really good. She slowly turned me over and I felt my nature rub up against her and it turned us both on. She sat up while I slid her night gown up a little. She sat back slowly as my nature entered her. She let out a low moan as she slowly moved her hips back and forth. She gently scratched her nails against my chest as I felt her juices start to slowly run down my waist. She started moving as if she was winding on me, that's when I felt like I was in true ecstasy, our bodies intertwined. I saw tears rolling down her face as she started moaning, *"I love you Sincere."* I took her by her hips and helped her wind. She grabbed my hands and helped me move her up, down, back, and forth. I took my hands and moved them up with the night gown until I had taken it off of Savannah. Now that she was naked, I started massaging her breasts. She moved closer to me and let me feel her body against mine. The sweat started to pour down our bodies. I started massaging her butt and gently grabbed it as I started to erupt like a volcano. *"I love you Savannah,"* I said with passion. *"I love you Sincere,"* Savannah returned in true bliss. I grabbed her hips and started moving her even faster. Savannah slowly laid down on me as she continued to wind her hips. She let out a faint cry as her juices started flowing once again. *"Oh shoot,"* I said suddenly. *"What, baby?"* Savannah said, startled and sitting up on me suddenly. *"I didn't put on a condom." "You can't be serious baby,"* Savannah slowly got off of me to see both her juices and the product of my eruption flowing out of her. She laid down on me. *"Maybe I won't get pregnant baby," "Hmmmmm, I don't know,"* I replied.

The doorbell rang and I opened the door; it was a middle-aged couple. *"Hi, we are Mr. and Mrs. Williams. You must be Sincere, is Savannah here?"* asked Mr. Williams. *"Oh, sure sir,"* I answered. *"Savannah,"* Mr. Williams called out looking around. Savannah came downstairs in black sweats and my gray Hofstra tee shirt with a few modifications that she made to it. She looked so good I wanted to put it on her again. She came down combing her hair. *"Hey Mom and Dad, how was your trip?"* Savannah asked. *"Fine baby. We were worried when we couldn't find you,"* Mr. Williams said. *"Oh, I didn't want to stay at that big house by myself so I asked Sincere if I could stay here with him. He is such a gentleman he offered me his room while he slept down here on the couch, making sure I slept safe and sound,"* Savannah answered her father. *"Thanks for taking care of my baby, Sincere."* Mrs. Williams said with a smile. *"Okay, I guess we can go across the street then,"* Mr. Williams stated. *"I'll be there in a sec Daddy,"* exclaimed Savannah. We hugged each other and said, *"I love you."* I gave her a big kiss on the cheek. *"Oh, Sincere, my mother said you have something to talk to me about?"* Mr. Williams said turning around with a concerned look on his face. *"Yes sir, but I'll let you get comfortable at the house and I'll come by and talk to you later,"* I answered. *"Okay, whenever you're ready, come on across the street,"* Mr. Williams answered back. *"Will do, sir."*

Before I went to Savannah's house, my phone rang, and it was my cousin Kaseem. *"What up fam?"* Kaseem asked. *"Nothing much, what's da deal with you?"* I answered back. *"Nuttin' what's going on down there?"* Kaseem asked. *"Nuttin really Jaheim, the crew and basically their whole family moved to*

*Alabama to be closer to their grandmother," I an-
swered. "Oh, cool, so how's it going with you and
Savannah?" Kaseem asked. "It's getting real serious, I'm thinking about popping the question," I
answered Kaseem. "Sin, I am glad to hear that, we
have been so worried about you. The family is going
to be ecstatic. I knew we made the right choice by
leaving the house to you so you could get a fresh
start. Big Mama would have wanted it this way. I
loved Cyan dearly trust me, but you had to move on
and live Sin for real. I know Cyan would have wanted
the same thing for you." "Ka, man look I think Savannah is pregnant." "Are you serious? Is that why
you are marrying her Sin?" "Na, man I was gonna
ask her to marry me anyway; just do me a favor and
don't say anything until we know for sure." "Yea,
fam you can count on me." "I'ight, lata Kaseem."
"Lata Sincere."*

I headed across the street go see Savannah's father. When I got over there Mrs. Williams was laying
across Mr. Williams' lap on their swinging chair.
When they saw me, they both smiled. Mrs. Williams
got up and walked into the house. *"Come here son
and have a seat,"* Mr. Williams said to me. I sat
down on the chair next to the swinging chair. *"My
daughter is crazy about you young man." "Yes, sir
and I'm crazy about her too." "What do you need to*

talk to me about?" "Well sir the time I have spent getting to know your daughter has really given me a new outlook on life. Savannah completes my heart. I know that may sound weird but…" "I know the feeling,"* Mr. Williams broke in, *"I feel that way about Savannah's mother,"* *"Okay well, that being the case will you give me your blessing to have your daughter as my wife?"* *"Whoa, that's a big step, are you sure that's what you want? How do you know that she is the one?"* *"Honestly, sir with all of her faults and flaws she is perfect to me and for me."* Savannah's father looked at me with an impressed look and then stated, *"So Savannah is like her mother and can have numerous emotions from one moment to the next."* *"I understand that sir but honestly if I can't love Savannah and be with her at her worst then I don't deserve to love and be with her at her best."* At that point Savannah's father said, *"That was only a test statement, but wow sounds like you are sure about this."* *"Sir I am very sure about this."* *"Okay so how will you provide for her?"* *"Well, actually I have my own school in New York; it's a day care and music school. I let my mother run it now and we split the profit. I'm working on opening a school here too. I was also thinking about opening a horse-riding academy, but I was actually looking for a partner to do that with."* *"Sincere, Savannah didn't mention* *that you like horses,"* *"Oh yes sir, I love horses."* *"Maybe we can go into business together son."* *"Wow so does this mean you will give me your blessing?"* *"Sure, as long as I know my baby will be taken care of and you do right by her, I have no problem."* We stood up and shook hands. *"Wait…Sincere,"* Mr. Williams said as I was walking away. *"Yes, sir?"* I asked, turning around. *"You look so familiar; did I meet you in New York?"* *"No not that I know of, but maybe."* Mr. Williams with a peculiar look on his face said *"humph"* shrugged his shoulders and said *"See you later, son"* with a big smile on his face.

FOUR

"Happy Birthday Baby!" Savannah said as she walked through the door. It was a crisp Autumn night with a beautiful full moon. It was early October which meant that the night would be still and quiet. Savannah waited for me to close the door. She had on a long gray dress which outlined each and every one of her curves. We popped popcorn and watched movies. I told Savannah I would take her home and she asked if she could just lay next to me for a bit. Me and Savannah agreed on a two-hour nap and then I would take her home. Well as soon as we got in my room, we started kissing. I slowly moved her shoulder straps down to her waist revealing her soft tender breasts as she unbuttoned my shirt and took it off of me. We pressed our bodies against each other. I slowly inched her dress up to her waist, she unbuttoned my pants and pushed them down, I stepped out of them and I slowly laid her back on the bed. We let our hands intertwine as I entered her soft, sweet, wet, and tender ocean of love. She squeezed my hand as she felt the pressure. I gave her soft and loving strokes as she pulled me closer to her. *"Baby I love*

you so much," Savannah whispered in my ear. *"I love you too Savannah."* Things started to heat up between us as Savannah's juices started to run continuously. When I thought she was done, her juices started flowing all over again. After about the sixth time that happened, I started thinking either she is extremely horny or there is something weird going on. I went with the thought of her being horny. I couldn't think too hard because Savannah started flowing again, and all I could think to myself was, this is beautiful and I am the man (okay, what dude would not think that at a time like this?). Savannah wrapped her legs around me and started to nibble on my ear. I felt my stomach tighten and my strokes began to pick up speed and become longer. As I started to explode Savannah started to softly whisper and cry my name at the same time. I gave Savannah a kiss. *"Baby it felt so good the last time that I didn't put a condom on this time."* *"Well baby,"* Savannah said as she looked into my eyes, *"It really doesn't make a difference, because I'm pregnant."*

The next day arrived bright and peaceful. Savannah rang my doorbell and greeted me with a hug and a kiss. *"Hey daddy."* *"What's up mama?"* *"Very nice birthday present, huh?"* *"Yea Savannah it's one of the best, I just hope I can do the same for you on yours."* *"Well, you only have a day Sincere."* *"Yea, I know we're two days apart, your birthday is tomorrow." 'Tell me honestly baby, how do you feel about becoming a father, are you ready?" 'Well truthfully I was asking to become a father by not putting on a condom. You not checking to see if we were protected also showed that you were asking to be a mother, so are you ready to be a mother?" "Yea, I was just worried because I didn't know how you felt about me being pregnant."* I took Savannah by the hands kissed them, looked into her eyes and said *"Baby, believe me I'm happy you're having my baby. I'll be here for you mentally, physically, spiritually, and every way that you need me to be. We're in this together, and I'm always here by your side."* At that Savannah sighed a sigh of relief and then asked, *"Are we good financially?" "Of course. Why are you asking?" "Well I know you had plans to open up another school and to build a horse stable to start a horse-riding academy."* I put Savannah's arms over my neck as I started to hug her by the waist and said, *"You know what baby, you're more important than all of that and don't you forget that."* Savannah smiled and hugged me tighter. I held her and kissed her on her neck.

Savannah's birthday was here. The ring that I had ordered for her was here and everything was perfect. Savannah rang the doorbell and I opened it and saw

Savannah wearing a thigh length black skirt with flowers on it. She also had on a black short sleeve shirt which made her breasts look very tempting. She walked in and ran her hand down my chest and on to my stomach. She whispered in my ear, *"I want you tonight."* *"But I thought we…"* *"Shhh"* Savannah covered my mouth. *"I want you to take me upstairs and I want it to be me and you all night long."* *"Baby you're pregnant."* *"Yea and I'm horny too."* Savannah took me over to an armless kitchen chair and sat me down. She took my hand and ran it up her leg, past her thigh and up in between her legs. She unbuttoned my shirt and pulled it off, ran her fingers around my neck and then she started to rub my chest. She worked her hands down to my pants, unbuttoned them and unzipped them. *"Baby what are you doing?"* I asked. *"It's my birthday so you have to grant all my wishes, so take off your pants."* I lowered my pants as Savannah ran her fingers over each one of the muscles on my stomach. *"Since you won't cooperate and take me upstairs, I'm just gonna take you right here."* *"Oh really?"* Savannah took my hands and had me move her skirt up to her waist; she sat down on my nature and let it slip inside of her. I put my hands around her waist and as she put her hands on the headrest of the chair she started moving up and down. I took my hands and started rubbing her thick, beautiful, luscious thighs and legs. I moved my hand up to her shirt and took it off her. I left her black bra on and kissed her breasts. I started kissing her on her neck and caressing her back. I started rubbing her spine; I moved my hands down to her waist and helped her with the motions of riding. Savannah started softly biting her lips, it looked so sexy. She gave a small giggle as her wetness started flowing down on the lower half of my body. Savannah's body started quivering and she started moaning as her love kept flowing out of her. I wrapped my hands underneath and over her shoulders as I started to slowly go deeper inside of her. She started moaning louder as our bodies started to melt into each other. I moved my hands down to her butt as I started to move faster and deeper. I gave her butt a soft squeeze as my stomach tightened and I started to explode inside of her. We started kissing and expressed our love for each other. She laid her head on my shoulders and I took my hands and started rubbing her all over her body. I looked over at the clock and it was 9:30 P.M. *"Savannah you see what time it is?"* *"Oh shoot we have to go Sin."* We got dressed and went across the street; her parents were sitting around waiting for us. *"Sorry we're late. It's my fault,"* I said to her parents. *"That's okay,"* Mrs. Williams said. Mr. Williams looked at his watch and then looked at me through his glasses while clearing his throat. They both had on robes; there was a cake on the table that said Happy Birthday Savannah. After blowing out her candles, Savannah ran up to her room to get something. I turned to her parents *"If it is okay with you, Savannah and I are gonna watch movies and hang out at my house." "Well both of you are grown but thanks for asking Sincere, that is a sign of a true gentleman."* Mr. Williams said with a smile on his face. Savannah came back down with a bag in her hand. *"Mom, Dad can I hang out with Sincere and just come home in the morning?" "Wait, we are just across the street...."* Mr. Williams started. *"Honey it is her birthday,"* Mrs. Williams cut in while giving Mr. Williams a look. Mr. Williams clearly catching the look stated, *"Well Savannah it's your birthday I guess it's okay, count this as one of your birthday presents." "Thank you, Mommy and Daddy."* Savannah kissed her parents and secretly gave her mother a high five. On our way out I whispered to Savannah, *"That was too easy," "No it wasn't,"* Savannah said through a smile while turning around to wave to her parents. *"They were wearing robes; that means they were doing the same thing we were and are going to continue doing tonight, my mother practically just kicked me out of the house, so they could have it all to themselves." "Ewww that's an over-share ma."* Savannah started giggling. We got back to my place and went upstairs to my room. I laid down in the bed and Savannah walked into the bathroom. She came out in this short silk black robe. She climbed on top of me and I clapped my hands twice. When I did this, my fireplace roared up and 112's "Sweet Love" started playing. *"Hmmm, interesting,"* Savannah exclaimed. I took off my shirt, laid back, and took off my shorts. I sat up towards her as she slid my rod of love in her then I laid her down on her back. I started to kiss her and tell her how much I love her. *"Savannah." "Yes baby,"* she said with a moan. *"Well, we've been together for a little over a year."* I took a breath (it's hard to talk while you're making love, I mean when it is really good, you're all out of breath and stuff). *"Baby, I just wanted to know if you would do me the honor of being my wife?"* Savannah looked at me as tears started rolling down the side of her eyes. *"Come here baby,"* Savannah kissed me and said, *"I would love to be your wife."* She held me close to her as more tears fell down her cheek. I slipped the 2 ½ carat diamond ring on her finger. The center diamond was princess while the surrounding diamonds were of different diamond cuts. We held each other for a while. I slid off of Savannah and took her to the end of the bed so we would be closer to the fire. I started kissing her on her back as she slid onto my rod again; she grabbed the back of my head as I started kissing the back of her neck. She slowly started moving up and down as I massaged her breasts and worked my way down in between her legs. She moaned from extreme pleasure. She started to slowly shiver as my body started to go numb. I felt this rush suddenly start to ball up inside of me. I opened Savannah's legs around mine and lifted her by the bottom of her legs and moved her up and down. I couldn't believe how great that felt. Savannah started moaning louder and I felt her start to drip and run down on me and that's when my rod of love erupted into Savannah. Savannah started to dig her nails into my leg as she moaned, and her body started to quiver. I gently moved her up and down as I kept feeling myself burst inside of her. We were both breathing heavily as Savannah eased herself up, turned around and we both moved to the head of the bed. I felt her body still quivering as she laid her head on my chest. She kept kissing me on my chest as I rubbed her head. I pulled her on top of me; she moved her legs all the way up to my waist and just laid on top of me. I started rubbing her whole body down as we fell asleep in each other's arms, both with smiles on our faces.

"Mom and Dad, look!" Savannah screamed while walking through her front door. *"What is it honey?"* asked Mrs. Williams. *"Sincere proposed to me last night,"* Savannah answered. *"Oh really? Come tell me how it all happened."* Savannah and her mother left the room. *"So, you popped the big question huh?"* Mr. Williams asked as he walked up to me with a big smile. *"Yea I did and I'm really happy I did."* *"I'm glad, because you've got yourself a great young woman and I'm sure she has herself a fine young man."* *"Thank you, sir."* Savannah and Mrs. Williams entered the room. *"Sincere that was so romantic how you proposed,"* Mrs. Williams stated. I took a deep gulp and looked at Savannah when I heard those words (No way; she didn't tell her mother, did she?). "Proposing during a nice romantic candlelit slow dance." I let out a breath of relief. *"Anything for my baby."* *"Sincere is something wrong? Your face looks like you saw a ghost or something,"* Mr. Williams stated to me. *"No when your wife said that statement the whole night replayed in my head."* *"Oh, okay."* Mr. Williams gave me a what-did-you-two-do last night look. Just then the doorbell rang, and Mr. Williams went to answer the door. Savannah hit me in the back of the head as she walked past and looked back at me. I shrugged my shoulders and whispered *"What?"* with a smirk

on my face. Mr. Williams opened the door and invited whoever it was in. As the couple started stepping into the house; I stood and stared in shock. *"What are you guys doing here?"* *"We wanted to come visit our son for his birthday and also meet this girlfriend of his that we've heard so much about."* My parents had come down from New York to see me. *"I missed you guys so much."* *"We've missed you too, son,"* my father answered back. *"Well Savannah's not my girlfriend anymore, she's my fiancée!"* *"Well then let me meet my future daughter-in-law!"* my mother said with excitement. First, *"Mr. and Mrs. Robinson meet Mr. and Mrs. Williams,"* I started introducing me and Savannah's parents. *"It's a pleasure to meet you,"* was exclaimed by both parties. My mother walked up to Savannah, put her hands on her face, kissed her on the cheek, hugged her and said, *"Welcome to the family sweetie."* *"So how long are you guys going to be here?"* *"Just the weekend,"* my father answered as he finished hugging Savannah. *"We would have been down here sooner, but I had meetings and your mother didn't want to close the school down."* *"What kind of work do you do Mr. Robinson?"* *"Oh no, please call me Marques. I am the CEO of Truly Blessed Productions and my wife Veronica runs the school that Sincere opened up...and you?"*

"Travis," Mr. Williams broke in. *"I just retired after 35 years with the Sheriff's Department in New York and my wife Patricia took the position of head accountant at U-Can-Count-On-Us Agencies." "Wow, that's great; we're all from New York. You know what, we're thinking about expanding our businesses and I am sure we probably could all work together somehow,"* Marques said. *"We are practically family now,"* Veronica said. *"You know that is a great idea, Veronica."* Patricia stated. *"Okay Savannah, you earned your bragging rights so come here and flash that big ol' rock for us,"* Veronica said. We all started laughing. My father pulled me aside gave me a hug and said, *"You did good son, you did good."* My mother joined us and said, *"I'm so proud of you baby."*

"Savannah, we need to tell them." "I know baby but how? They are gonna think that's the only reason why you want to marry me." "Why would you think that Savannah?" "Let's see, you asked me to marry you on my birthday and now I'm magically two months pregnant. What would you think if our kids came up to us with the same scenario?" "I would say hey you sound just like me and your moms about 20 years ago." "That's not funny Sin, this is serious," Savannah couldn't help but chuckle and shake her head. *"I know baby, but what's done is done; we've*

got to make the best of it.” That night after we ate dinner together our families sat down in Savannah's living room. *“We have something to tell you guys,”* I started. *“What's up? Talk to us,”* Marques said. Veronica and Patricia looked at us both kind of sideways and then looked at each other and both said *“Oh, no!”* Then Marques and Travis looked at our mothers, looked at each other and then looked at us and said, *“What?”* But it was one of those “I know it's not what I think it is” kind of what. Savannah put her head down and Patricia immediately said, *“Why are you dropping your head down?”* My mother asked, *“Are y'all getting married because of this baby?”* *“No, mama, I wanted to ask Savannah to marry me before we found out that she was pregnant.”* *“How did you guys let this happen?”* Patricia asked us. *“Mama it just happened, there is no excuse,”* Savannah answered. *“You know there's an aisle of nothing but protection at the store; you mean to tell me you just happened to miss it? I mean did I miss the wedding or something, hello?”* my mother said looking at the both of us. *“I know mama,”* I answered. *“Well obviously you didn't know, since you got Savannah pregnant,”* my mother said back, very angry. *“How far along are you?”* Patricia asked. *“Two months mama,”* Savannah answered her mother. *“Two months? You kept this from us until now?"* Patricia fired back. *"I am not trying to make any excuses, but they are both grown, they are not teenagers. We are talking about two grown adults who have finished college and have careers. Yelling definitely isn't going to solve anything,"* my father chimed in, soothing my mother. *"A baby is a big responsibility; you know that right son?"* Travis asked. *"Yes sir, I know. I love your daughter and she means everything to me and I want to spend the rest of my life with her." "You don't even know about life yet,"* Patricia blurted out. *"Well who are we to judge? Marques is right, they are not little kids, they are grown adults and we are treating them like teenagers,"* my mother stated. *"Well, umm...you're right Veronica,"* Patricia said stuttering over her words. *"Well you have our permission and blessing, so I have no doubt that everything will be fine,"* Travis stated with confidence. *"First you get engaged and now you tell us you're two months pregnant. Wow a grandchild,"* my mother said in amazement and excitement. *"I hope you two are ready, because I don't plan on raising grandchildren too; this child is your responsibility,"* Patricia added. *"Umm we never asked you to raise our child mama; we are both adults and can hold our own,"* Savannah blurted back, with her feelings hurt. I put my arm around her, kissed her on the cheek and softly whispered in her ear, *"Everything is going to be fine; I don't want you to worry about anything."* "Patricia let it go, she's not a baby. She is our grown daughter. They can take care of themselves and a baby," Travis stated trying to soothe Patricia.

"Call me when you guys get back to New York," I said to my parents as I waved to them and they pulled off to start their journey back home. What a weekend! It was still early so I decided to take a nap. I woke up to find Savannah in my arms. I softly whispered to her, *"How did you get in here?"* *"Oh, your mother gave me a copy of the house key. She said I'm family now and she really doesn't want you to be in the house by yourself; she said you've been lonely for too long. She recommended that I keep you company as much as I can. I'm taking her up on her advice."* *"Oh really?"* I asked. Savannah started rubbing her butt into my pelvis. *"Baby you need to stop; that's exactly why you are pregnant now,"* I said. *"No, I'm pregnant because you were too horny to put on a condom,"* Savannah said back jokingly. *"Come on baby, just for a little while, what you afraid I'm going to get pregnant? I think it's a little too late for that baby."* *"Ha ha ha so funny, I see you got jokes,"* I started tickling Savannah. *"Stop you're going to make me pee on myself,"* she half screamed, and half laughed. I pulled her close to me and started

kissing her on the back of her neck. *"I love you baby,"* I whispered. She reached back and started rubbing me on the back of my neck. *"I love you too honey."* I moved my arms down to her stomach and she moved her hands on top of mine. We fell asleep holding each other.

Savannah woke me up with a kiss and asked, *"Do you regret anything Sincere?" "I don't regret us; I don't regret asking you to marry me and I don't regret getting you pregnant. I have absolutely no regrets. Why what's wrong Savannah?" "Nothing really, I just wonder sometimes." "I don't see you any differently; I love you like I loved you before, in fact I love you even more. You have nothing to worry about okay?"* Savannah leaned over on me and I kissed her on her head. I held her in my arms as we fell back asleep.

"Hello?" I said while reaching for the clock, which said 5:12 P.M. *"Ay, yo Sin, what up?"* said the voice on the other end of the phone. *"What up Ka?" "Tell Kaseem we're trying to get some sleep,"* said Savannah yawning. *"What's up Ka, what's wrong man?" "Ay yo Sin man I'm wildin' out you'll never believe what I did." "What did you do now man?" "Do you remember Ashley Martin?" "Yeah,"* I said with extreme concern. *"Well, me and her kept in touch throughout the years. So, I met up with her at*

our Pops' record label; because there was a job opening." "Okay what's your point?" "Well your Pops made me in charge of the hiring." "Okay so?" "Well Ashley and I were in my office and I gave her the interview and then we started flirting with each other." "No tell me you didn't Ka." "Yeah man, had sex right there on my desk." "No, tell me you're playing." "Yo, Sin she had on this shirt that emphasized her breasts. I mean the shirt made her breasts look like they were trying to bust out. The skirt she was wearing showed her curves to the fullest. Her legs looked so sexy and her butt was definitely on point." "So, what happened? I said, very disappointed. *"Well like I said we were flirting, and she told me how she still loved me after all these years."* "Whoa, she gamed you for the job," I broke in. *"Yo, Sin I don't care cause I got some free play for it, anyway like I was saying she got up and walked over towards me and leaned over me pushing her breasts all up in my face. I started rubbing on her thighs as she was pulling down my zipper. I lifted her up, put her on top of the desk and then went to work banging her back out." "Come on man, that's an over share Ka, I don't need to know all of that,"* I said with extreme disgust. *"My bad Sin,"* Kaseem said laughing and then went on. *"Yo, but don't get me wrong she was already qualified for the job before anything happened." "Oh, I'm sure she was, Ka. Even if she wasn't, I'm sure her giving it up to you helped out a whole lot didn't it?"* I said sarcastically. *"Come on Sin, you know it's nothing like that."* Savannah got up, reached over me and grabbed the phone and said, *"Kaseem, really? Do not corrupt my man with your sexcapades and I also hope you were protected. Now let Sincere go back to sleep." "I'm sorry darling I'll be done with him in a sec and then he's all yours,"* Kaseem said to Savannah in his sweetest voice. *"Whatever,"* was Savannah's reply while giggling. Savannah then got up and went into the bathroom to take a shower. I got back on the phone with Kaseem, *"Sin, Ashley's body is still on point. Cuz her butt is like an onion. When I saw it, I wanted to cry." "You're so stupid Kaseem,"* I said back laughing. *"Anyway, Ashley is my personal secretary since that was the job opening that was being offered." "Oh, how convenient, huh Ka?" "Yeah I guess so Sin, anyway after everything was done, we were talking, and we started talking about you." "Why?"* I asked. *"Oh, Ashley just wanted to know how you were doing and everything, then she told me to tell you her sister Alana said hi and that she misses you."* At that moment, my mouth flew open because I knew this was coming once he mentioned Ashley.

Alana Martin, wow I haven't seen her since I left New York, in fact she was the last person I saw when I left New York. I saw her as I was heading to the airport. Luckily, she did not see me. Last time I saw Alana she had long black hair with red highlights and it's naturally curly like Ashley's. Alana's body was definitely on point. Her body was so tight that she could silence a room when she walked in. She had a real natural beauty to her. A mocha complexion, nice slightly oval eyes and nice kissable lips. The only difference with Ashley is she is slightly darker than Alana. The Martin sisters were a heartbreaking pair and what made it worse was they were only 10 months apart. Yeah, their parents were definitely bumping – n – grinding having them girls back to back.

"Ay yo by the way Sin, " Kaseem said breaking up my daydream. *"What up Ka?"* *"I gave Ashley your number to give to Alana."* *"Why did you do that, you know I'm engaged to Savannah and you know me and Savannah are having a baby. What's wrong with you man, what were you thinking? Do you not re-member the history between me and Alana?"* I said angrily. *"Sin, Alana just wants to say hi."* *"Yea, I'm sure she does Kaseem, I'll holla at you later fam."* *"I'ight later Sin."* *"Wait Ka,"* *"Yea, Sin"* *"weren't you engaged, what happened to the one you were*

with for two years?" "Yea we had so many issues that I had to end it today." "Ummm, so technically you were still engaged while getting it in with Ash-ley?" "Well, yea I broke it off after Ashley left my office." "How convenient, you know what cuz? I do not want to hear anything else. I am not going to be an accomplice in your shenanigans." "Later Ka." "Later, Sin." Dang, I don't want Alana having my phone number. Alana and Cyan hated each other. Alana was always trying to push up on me and Cyan always shut her down. I had to prevent Cyan numer-ous times from giving Alana the worst beat down of her life.

FIVE

I met the Martin sisters back in high school. They had just moved into town. In high school I was an undercover nerd. Very popular, class clown, but when it came to tests, I was like a super genius. I was classified as one of the coolest student coordinators. When Ashley and Alana got to the school, I was the one who had to show them around and everything like that. Cyan and I were patching things up after a huge argument that we recently had. We would still talk and kick it, but we were both hurting and took a little time apart. Anyway, Alana took a real liking to me and since the unemployed Kaseem kept "vacationing" with my family in New York, I hooked him up with Ashley. The deal with Kaseem was that he graduated from high school early. He was supposed to play football for Virginia Tech but shattered his knee in a car accident and lost his scholarship. He had been depressed ever since, so he never returned to school. Anyway, the relationship between Alana and I was strictly on a friendship level. I told her I was seriously involved with someone and she and I could only be friends. Alana took that for a while, but then she wanted more. One day Alana and Ashley came to my house. Kaseem and I were chilling in my basement apartment when my doorbell rang. I let the girls in. We were chilling watching T.V. when Ashley and Kaseem got up and went into the guest bedroom which was pretty much his room anyway. Alana and I were watching T.V. when she moved in closer to me and she tried to kiss me on my neck. At first, I kept telling her we couldn't, she kept trying and then I got turned on and started kissing her on her neck. I started sliding my hand up her thigh. Alana tried stopping me and telling me how I was right and that we shouldn't do anything. I stopped but I guess we were both heated and we looked at each other and started kissing. I don't know how but somehow it happened anyway right there on the couch. Alana and I had sex; we both couldn't believe what happened, and we kept asking each other about it as she laid on my chest. At first, we tried to keep it a secret. Through the months Alana and Ashley came to my house constantly and the same thing happened but instead of on the couch Alana and I had sex in my bedroom. The very last time we did it, me and Alana fell asleep and we spent the night together. By then Kaseem and Ashley knew me and Alana were having sex on a regular basis. The morning we woke up together, I told Alana we couldn't do it anymore.

She agreed and that was that. Kaseem was in love with Ashley and he decided it was time to get his life back on track. Unfortunately, he was going back to VA. He did promise Ashley that he would come back for her. Even though it broke Ashley's heart, she understood. Well, Cyan and I worked things out and got back together. One day while I was chilling, eating lunch with Cyan, Alana approached us. Cyan looked up and was like *"Hi, how are you?"* Alana said *"Fine,"* and then stated, *"I know you really don't know me all that well but me and my sister really don't have any friends. We were wondering if we could hang out with you?"* Cyan said, *"sure"* and that was that. Alana turned to me and gave me the most evil smile and look in the world.

Alana, Ashley, and Cyan would go shopping at the mall and things like that. Cyan actually started trusting them. One day we were all in the office with the principal and the mediators/deans of the school, brainstorming on different ideas. All of a sudden Alana said, *"Cyan, do you know Sincere is the sweetest person?"* Cyan said *"Yes, that's why we're still together after so long."* Cyan took my hand and laid her head on my shoulder. Alana then said, *"Oh yeah y'all been together for a long time, but did Sincere tell you how we were together too?"* Cyan looked at Alana and said, *"What did you say?"* Cyan then looked at me with tears forming in her eyes and asked, *"Is that true?"* *"Uh...Uh.... Ab.... Ab..."* is all I could say, the words just would not come out, I just dropped my head. Cyan started crying. *"Now kids calm down we can work this out,"* said Principal Johnson. *"No Sincere, I hate you and I never want to be with you again."* Those words delivered a deadly blow to my heart. Cyan walked out. Alana looked at me, gave me that devilish grin and walked out. Cyan wouldn't talk to me at all. Alana constantly tried to get with me, but I kept shutting her down. Cyan wouldn't take my phone calls; she wouldn't even look at me. One day I finally had her cornered; she was talking to Billy Mays, the school's star quarter-back. *"Take a hike B,"* I said. *"No, I'm not your girl anymore Sincere, just go away,"* Cyan said without even looking at me. *"You heard the girl Sin, beat it."* *"Look Billy don't act tough if you still want to play football, because you step to me and something bad is going to happen."* *"Oh yeah like what?"* Billy put his hand on my shoulder, and I caught hold of it and twisted it to the point where one little budge would break it. *"Come on man let go that's my throwing arm,"* Billy said through clenched teeth. *"Not anymore,"* I said back. I was going to deal the final blow when I heard Cyan crying saying, *"Stop it Sincere, why do you have to be such a jerk?"* I saw the tears of frustration in Cyan's eyes and I immediately let go of Billy's arm. He walked past me and pushed me with his shoulder, kissed Cyan on the cheek and told her he would see her later. *"You act so childish,"* Cyan said while shoving me away from her. She started to walk away when I caught her arm; she pulled herself away from me. *"Get off me, we're not together anymore, why don't you run to Alana?"* *"Cyan I made a mistake, I give you that, but we've been together since we were kids. We can't let that just die."* *"Oh really? Why didn't you think of that before you started sleeping with Alana?"* At that, tears started to slowly flow from Cyan's eyes. *"Sincere we were each other's first, how could you go and share our love with someone else?"* *"Cyan I'm sorry; I would take it back if I could. I promise it will never happen again."* Cyan looked at me and said, *"You know you're right; it won't ever happen again because I won't be around for you to ever do that to me again."* *"Cyan wait, I love you."* *"Oh yeah? Well it's too late for that, even if we were spending time apart you should have come to me. I needed you not her."* *"So, what are you saying Cyan?"* The words balled up in my throat. *"You should have been sleeping with me and not her, I was your woman not her. Even if we didn't sleep together you should have just come to me and not her. It's okay though I won't think of you while I'm wrapped up in Billy's arms tonight!"* At that Cyan walked away.

That night while I was chilling on the couch, my doorbell rang. I opened it and it was Cyan. She walked in and said *"Hello."* I replied the same. *"What's up, you coming to brag about what you just finished doing with Billy?"* I said sarcastically. *"That's not important. I came to talk to you,"* Cyan replied with a smile. *"I actually just did come from seeing Billy. I told him although he is a great guy, I'm in love with you, Sincere and even though you are a jerk and you hurt me so bad, I still love you."* My heart jumped for joy and felt crushed at the same time. *"We need to seriously talk Sincere because you really hurt me. Why did you do it Sincere, why couldn't you have just come to me?"* *"Look Cyan I made a very stupid mistake and you're right; I should have come to you."* *"Sincere do you still have feelings for her?"* *"No,"* I said instantly. Cyan looked at me, searched my eyes, and was satisfied. *"So, does this mean we are back together Cyan?"* *"I don't know, you tell me Sincere."* *"Cyan I don't want to live without you."* *"Tough, you should have thought about that before you did what you did."* *"What?"* I asked. Cyan totally surprised me with that outburst. Cyan looked down and then replied, *"I don't want to live without you either, but I have to know that I can trust you, so you're on probation until further notice." "Okay that's fair Cyan."* I went to give Cyan a kiss, but she backed up and said *"no, you have not earned that yet."* My house phone rang and I went to pick it up, but Cyan grabbed the phone. *"Hello,"* Cyan said, then started giggling. *"No check this out, you already know who it is and you are calling my man's house. I advise you to stop calling here before something bad happens."*

From that day on it was war. Every time Alana tried to break me and Cyan up it failed because we had a deeper love for each other, and I wasn't going to lose Cyan again. I got a second chance and doubted I would get another one if I messed up again. Cyan was happy that she had a reason to beat Alana down and I was trying to prevent that from happening ever since, especially since I couldn't beat down Billy Mays. As for Billy Mays, he graduated, went to Grambling State University on a full scholarship and married the head cheerleader. Anyway, I remember one time before graduation, Cyan and Alana were in the hallway arguing. Normally a guy would be ecstatic to see two girls fighting over him and for a second, I was (such a guy huh?). Anyway, someone came to me and told me what was going on, so I had to run to where they were. By the time I got there, there was a huge crowd around Cyan and Alana in addition to the crowd following me. I heard Cyan screaming, *"He's my man and don't get yourself hurt."* Alana screamed back, *"Whatever; I guess we will see about that."* Just as Cyan raised her fist, I stepped in between them, grabbed Cyan, kissed her, picked her up and carried her away. Cyan was mad at me, but I told her it wasn't worth it. Cyan told me I should have just let her knock Alana out.

Savannah woke me up with a kiss on the cheek. *"What's wrong baby?"* Savannah asked. *"Nothing baby, just had a weird dream,"* I answered back. Kaseem just had to meet back up with Ashley when he moved to New York. I bet Alana has been on a mission to get me back once she heard that Cyan died. I won't let Alana ruin me and Savannah's relationship. Savannah got dressed and went home to spend time with her parents. It was 9:30 P.M. and I was sitting on the couch watching T.V. when the phone rang. *"Hello."* *"Hey Sincere I haven't heard from you in a long time, did you forget about me?"* *"Alana?"* I said surprised. *"Yea baby how did you know it was me?"* Alana answered back just as surprised. *"Kaseem told me you had my number."* *"Oh, okay so what's up?"* Alana asked. *"Listen Alana, I'm engaged and I'm about to be a father. What me and you had was back in high school and that's that. Nothing is going to happen between me and you."*

"I'm sorry about Cyan; Sincere I know your heart must be broken." I know she did not just try to act like she didn't hear a word I said. *"If you need any-thing, you give me a call alright Sincere? I love you, bye bye now."* Click…. did that chick just hang up on me ignoring every word I said? I hurried up and called Kaseem. *"He…."* *"Kaseem call Ashley three way,"* I broke in before he could fully get a word out. *"Why what's…"* *"Call her now Kaseem,"* I said in-terrupting again. *"Alright, alright,"* The phone rang. *"He…"* *"Hey Ashley, it's Sincere,"* I said cutting Kaseem off once again. *"Hey Sincere, how are you?"* *"I'm alright."* *"Hey baby,"* Kaseem finally got a word in. *"Hey baby what's up?"* *"Hey Ashley, can you put Alana on the phone please,"* I blurted out before Kaseem could answer. *"Sure,"* I heard Ashley call Alana. Alana came to the phone. *"Hello."* *"Listen you little she-devil. I'm about to be married. Your little high school game is not going to work."* *"Look Sincere what's up with the name call-ing? I heard all you had to say; but check this, nothing and I mean nothing is going to stop me from taking what is rightfully mine."* *"What do you mean rightfully yours?"* *"Well Cyan took you away from me, making me second in line and now that she's gone, you're all mine."* *"Are you delusional or something?"* *"Sincere you took my virginity and you*

had sex with me on multiple occasions including all of the oral action that went on between us too. I love you and we will be together no matter what. " At that Alana hung up the phone. *"What did you do to her Sin? You turned that freak out, "* Kaseem said laughing. "Yo, Ka that's not funny," I said angrily. *"Well at least I didn't get the psychotic one, "* Kaseem said laughing even louder. *"Ka man I got a serious problem on my hands, you know what I'm not even going to worry about it, it's not like she knows where I live or anything, " "Yo Sin, she already has your address." "What? "* I screamed in the phone and then I heard Kaseem's phone go dead.

My phone rang. *"Hello!"* I screamed angrily. *"Hey? Baby? Is everything alright? I called to check on you." "Yea Savannah I'm fine. What's up with you?" "Nothing, just called to see how you're doing, but I have to go finishing talking to my mother, I'll call you back in a few, love ya." "Love ya too mama. "* We both hung up. As soon as I put my phone down it rang. *"Hello." "Yo man they knew my address from when I moved down there remember?" "Oh yeah, you're right I ain't mad at ya Ka. I wish I never met her now man." "I feel ya Sin, but on a side note I want you to be the best man at me and Ashley's wedding." "You're going to marry Ashley?" "Yea I'm taking it as a sign from GOD. Ashley and I were apart for years, but now we're back together." "Al-right whatever makes you happy Ka, that's not my problem though; I don't want Alana coming down here and messing up my life with Savannah." "Yeah I know man,"* Kaseem replied *"Hey Sin, remember the time Cyan caught Alana outside of your house?" "Which time Kaseem?" "All of them," "I thought Cyan was gonna kill that girl." "Yea tell me about it Ka."*

One time Cyan and I were hanging out at my place and someone kept ringing my phone and hanging up, then a chick called and said, *"I'm watching you."* Cyan went and grabbed my baseball bat, opened my door and saw Alana sitting in her car. Cyan walked towards the car with the baseball bat, but Alana pulled off before Cyan got to her. *"This is all your fault Sincere; you should have never got involved with her,"* Cyan said. *"I know baby let's just go back inside."*

Just then I heard Kaseem's next question, *"Sin, you ever regret getting Savannah pregnant?" "Na, I mean we knew what could have happened and we took a chance anyway. You know what I'm saying Kaseem?" "Yea, but are you sure you want to marry her?" "Yea, I sure am, I'm not marrying Savannah just because she's pregnant. It's not like I'm getting married to her tomorrow, I mean we got time." "Yea fam I got worried about that, I thought you were marrying her because of the baby." "Na Ka, you know that's not my style." "I hear ya fam, ay yo I got to bounce. Ashley's calling me on the other line." "Ok fam, holla whenever." "Okay, lata Sin." "Lata."*

My phone rings. *"Hello,"* I answered sleepily while fumbling around for my clock - 4:10 A.M. *"Hey sexy, were you sleeping?"* a sexy voice answered back. *"Alana are you kidding me, don't you ever go to sleep?"* *"Na baby I'm horny and I can't stop thinking about you,"* she answered back. *"Sorry to hear that. Unfortunately, I still can't do anything about that."* *"Why not? You're not married yet,"* Alana answered back with an attitude. *"Remember the way we were watching T.V. and you leaned over and pulled me close to you? I was lying on your chest and when I looked up at you, you softly started to kiss me?"* *"What's your point Alana?"* I asked, ignoring her question. Alana went on *"and then you laid me back on the couch and started to kiss me? At first you played hard to get, but I'm glad you came out of your shell. Sincere it felt so good being with you. I loved when you started to take my shirt off and I was playing hard to get, but when you started kissing me on my neck it felt so good that I had to give in. You started kissing my breasts and sucking on my nipples. Then you started kissing my stomach and unbuttoning my pants. You took off my pants and started kissing my thighs and legs. You took my panties off and started kissing in between my thighs. You got me a cover because I told you I was cold. You were such a gentleman and so romantic."* "Alana," I broke in. *"What are you telling me this for? It's over and done with."* Once again ignoring me, Alana went on, *"I took your shirt off, took your pants off, boxers, and then pulled you close on top of me. When I told you I was a virgin, you were gentle with me like I was a delicate flower. You started to enter me and when the pain started, I squirmed and moaned. It was cute how you asked me if I wanted you to stop. I told you no, and you kept going very slow and soft. With each squirm you held me closer and closer comforting me. When you made it all the way, it was kind of a relief for the both of us. You made love to me so passionately. My first time was so beautiful; you held me as I cried in your arms. It was so beautiful. In fact, every time we made love it was like our very first time except the pain was less and less until there was finally no more."* *"Alana those days are done,"* I broke in once again. *"Sincere they don't have to be; can't you see how great we are together?"* *"Alana, I have moved on, I'm over you and it's time for you to do the same." "Well, I'm not over you Sincere and I will do whatever I have to do in order for us to be together, even if that means killing your fiancée."* Alana hung up the phone. Whoa, what did she just say? Alana has completely lost it. What am I going to do?

"Ay yo Ka, what kind of havoc did you release on my life?" "What are you talking about Sin?" "Yo Alana called me up first getting herself off over the phone and now she talking about killing Savannah." "What!!!!!!" exclaimed Kaseem in total shock. *"Yea man, Alana told me that she is going to kill Savannah in order for me and her to be together." "Whoa fam that is bugged out." "Ka, I have to protect Savannah man, yo she is having my kid and I'll kill Alana before I let her hurt Savannah or my baby." "Ay yo I feel ya Sin." "Man, I just wanted you to know what the deal is. Tell Ashley that she needs to have a talk with her sister." "Sin you got it."* At that we both said, *"Lata."*

Thanksgiving was here and both families were together. Jaheim, Khalil, Ray, Roscoe, Aunt Catherine, Mama Jo, everyone was together. After we ate dinner, we all went into the family room to play some family games. As soon as we got into the room Savannah and I stood in front of the family. *"Okay so we have an announcement,"* I started. *"Yes, Savannah and I are engaged."* At that point Savannah put her ring on and flashed it so everyone could see it. There were very positive responses. *"Thank you everyone, but wait there is more." "We have a little one on the way."* It was silent for a little while as everyone looked at each other around the room. *"Who wants dessert?"* Patricia asked trying to break the silence. Travis chimed in, *"We knew about it and we were just as surprised as everyone else, but they are grown, and I believe everything will be fine."* Mama Jo stated, *"A baby is a blessing, no murmurs or nothing, they are grown and have to handle this together. We are a family and we support each other. Nothing negative will be said, is that understood?"* There was a unison response of *"yes ma'am." "Now Savannah you come give your Gran Gran a hug and a kiss and tell me about your engagement and my great grandchild." "If it was anybody else, they would probably be seriously hurt,"* Jaheim said as we were sitting around the card table playing spades. *"You are so lucky it's you bro,"* Khalil stated. *"Thanks fellas I really appreciate it,"* I said, laughing. *"Wow, Sin is going to officially be one of us,"* Ray said to Roscoe. *"Welcome to the fam Sin,"* Roscoe stated to me. *"Thanks guys I really appreciate it, if we are all done being mushy now, someone needs to hurry up and lose so they can give up their seat in the game."* We all started laughing.

One day during the Christmas/New Year season, me and Savannah were chilling at my house and my phone rang. Savannah picked it up and whoever was on the other end hung up the phone. *"Wow, that's strange, hmm let me *69 and see who is playing games on your phone."* Savannah called the number back and said, *"Hello, did someone just call this number?"* The person on the other end of the phone said, *"I was looking for my man."* Savannah stated, *"Well this is my fiancé's house, so I think you have the wrong number."* *"I don't think so because I am looking for Sincere and I know this is his number."* Savannah looked at me and covered the phone and said, *"Who is this and what is she talking about you are her man?"* I hung up the phone and said, *"That is Alana, a girl from high school, who has a weird crush on me. Kaseem is with her sister and he gave her my number thinking that she and I were still friends."* *"Why does she think you are in a relation-ship, have you had conversations?"* Savannah said with an angry look on her face. *"She and I had a fling back in the day."* *"What do you mean a fling? Oh, you mean to tell me you slept with her?"* Savannah broke in. *"Yea back in high school I slept with her. She and I broke it off when Cyan and I were getting* *back together. Now that Cyan is out of the picture, she thinks I am rightfully hers."* "Oh, now does she?" Savannah pointed her finger at me, gave me a look that I will never forget and said, *"I will deal with you in a minute."* At that moment looking in Savannah's eyes I got a flash of Cyan. I snapped out of it as Savannah picked up the phone and *69 Alana again as she started pacing back and forth. *"I know you didn't..."* Alana started. *"Listen here I don't know what your little problem is, Sincere is my man, we are getting married and I am having his baby and that's that, whatever you thought you had is over."* *"Humph, like I told Sincere sweetie, I will do whatever I have to do to get him even if that means taking you out of the picture. I'm sure you know about Cyan, wouldn't want the same to happen to you."* *"Is that a threat Alana? You know what, bring it then because you will never have Sincere, he is all mine."* At that Savannah hung up the phone. Savannah looked at me and said, *"I need to sit down."* As she was sitting down, she asked, *"How long were you going to keep this from me Sincere?"* *"I told her never to call me again and pretty much told her all contact was over."* *"You never told me she called you Sincere, why?"* *"She is not important Savannah, you are."* *"Well I think you not hiding things is what's more important, how am I supposed to feel* *knowing that some girl you slept with has been call-ing you and wants a relationship with you?" "You are right, I messed up. I won't hide anything from you." "You better not Sin." "Ok babe."*

After that things had been going pretty good. I did not hear from Alana again after Savannah called her. Hopefully Kaseem and Ashley talked to her too. Well Kaseem and Ashley announced their engage-ment, so plans were underway for that, especially planning Kaseem's bachelor party.

"What's up sexy?" I asked Savannah. *"There is nothing sexy about me, I'm a big fat elephant,"* re-plied Savannah. *"No, you're not; your cravings have not been all that bad. You wanted a cheeseburger from Chico's Diner, a hero from Benny's Deli, Slurpees and that's about it." "Yea, but now look at me, I'm humongous." "No, you're not, you do not eat that much and even your doctor told you, you ha-ven't gained that much weight. She says that you are a perfectly normal size." "Well, the doctor is not the one carrying this baby." "Baby, you look so sexy, wanna go make love?"* I said giggling. *"Ewww, you want to make love to me looking like this?"* Savan-nah said in disgust. I said, *"Oh yeah,"* as I pulled her close to me and started kissing her. *"Thank you for being so nice to me even though, I know you don't find me attractive." "Savannah you are having my*

baby and believe me, the moment we can, I'm going to show you how much I appreciate you." "Yea just make sure you don't get me pregnant when I go back for my six-week checkup." I started laughing at that. *"What? That's not funny it has happened to a lot of people,"* Savannah replied. *"I have to prepare for one; you think I am ready for another one?"* I answered. *"You get so horny, who knows? Just make sure you're not too horny to put on a condom until I start taking the pill for at least a month." "Okay, deal baby."* I replied. *"I mean it baby,"* Savannah said back with a stern look. *"Okay you got it baby, I promise,"* I replied.

"Well let's begin the countdown," my mother said while handing me her bags. *"Tell me about it,"* I said back to my mother. *"So, are you ready son?"* my father asked. *"Oh, most definitely dad,"* I replied. *"Now you can see what I went through with you,"* my father said laughing. *"Oh, come on dad I wasn't that bad...was I?" "Humph, you have no idea son." "Oh, stop it Marques. Sincere, your father cried when you were born and carried you everywhere showing you off. You are your father's best friend, don't let him fool you." "Thank you, Mama." "Son, I just want you to know there was never a day where I wasn't proud of you." "Aww, thanks dad, don't get mushy on me now." "Men always try to hide their*

emotions." "Oh, mama cut it out, I'm proud of my father too, I wouldn't wish for anyone else, I wouldn't have anyone else as my parents, I love you both." "Aww we love you too son." "Okay well I'm going to see Patricia, I'll see you two guys later," my mother said while walking out of the door. *"Okay mama,"* I replied. *"Okay sweetheart,"* my father replied.

"Do you think they are going to be alright Veronica?" "Patricia, they'll be fine." "Veronica, I just worry about them so much," "Well GOD would not put more on them than they could bear so they will be fine, Patricia." "Can you believe that we are going to be grandmothers?" Patricia asked. *"Yea, I know isn't it amazing?"* Veronica replied. *"It feels like Sincere was just born yesterday and now he is going to be a father." "I know! I feel like I was just holding Savannah in my arms and then watching her play jump rope, now she is going to have a child of her own."* Patricia's eyes started filling up with tears. Veronica touched Patricia's hand and said, *"I know it hurts, but let's not be disappointed or angry for their sake." "I know I just didn't want it to be like this for them,"* Patricia answered. *"I wanted things to be different for them too Patricia, but they both made a decision that they have to live with." "Veronica, I wish they included us in their decision."*

"Well Patricia, our babies are not babies anymore, we raised them the best we could." "You're right Veronica; well I guess we just have to get ready to be grandmothers." "Patricia can you believe that our grandbaby will be here soon? I remember when they first told us and now Savannah is almost nine months pregnant." At that Veronica and Patricia hugged each other.

"Marques, I'm really not ready to be a grandfather." "You? Travis, you have no idea, my little boy's going to be a father." "Marques you got it easy, daddy's little girl is going to be a mother." "Travis you are right, I do have it easy." "What can we really say; at least they weren't young teenagers." "You're right Marques, but I always wanted her to get married first, not be like her mother and me. I took my job to support her and my wife, I gave up my dreams, and I struggled to put Patricia through school so she wouldn't have to give up her dreams, I just don't get it Marques." "Well Travis, we know what we had to do to raise our kids right, there is so much they don't know, but it's a secret that we hold that makes it all worthwhile. I commend Sincere for getting an early start on his business, yes, a tragedy occurred in his life, but Savannah helped him through it. Okay, so things didn't turn out the way that we wanted it to but trust me it could be

worse." "Marques, you're right it could be." "There was a time when Sincere's mother got really sick. Sincere gave up his scholarship and turned down so many opportunities just to stay by her side. His mother means more to him than anything in this world. When I was in the hospital he flew back home just to be by my side. My son is a good man and will do right by your daughter. I'm glad he is still alive, because for a long time he begged GOD to let him and Cyan trade places, he wished he had died instead of Cyan." "I don't doubt Sincere is a good man, I can see how you raised him, I just get worried sometimes. I wasn't ready for my little girl to grow up so fast." "Travis I wasn't ready for my little boy to grow up so fast." "Well Marques, looks like we are family now." At that point Marques and Travis shook hands.

"Okay, it's kind of weird Sin, our mothers are in one room talking and our fathers are in another room talking, what's going on?" "Savannah, I don't know, but at least they are getting along." "Well they have liked each other from the start Sin, so that hasn't been a problem, it's just weird. I wonder what they are talking about?" "Whatever it is, it's all good things Savannah," I said while giving her a kiss on the forehead. *"Oh, Wow!" "What Savannah?"* I asked frantically like Savannah just went into labor.

"The baby is up," Savannah said with a smile on her face. *"Oh,"* I said while letting out a sigh of relief. *"Don't scare me like that girl." "Well, you're the one that's all jumpy, do you see how calm I am? Well come over here daddy and say hello to your son or daughter." "You sure you still don't want to know whether we are having a boy or girl Savannah?" "No, I think we should both be surprised." "Okay,"* I said while placing my hands on Savannah's stomach and kissing it. *"I love it when you kiss my stomach,"* Savanna said softly. *"Well, my child is in there and I want my child to know how much I love him or her, even before he or she comes into the world." "Your baby loves you too." "Baby, how are you feeling?" "Sin I am fine; you don't have to worry about me." "No, Savannah, how are you feeling...for real?"* Savannah searched my eyes and saw how concerned I was and said, *"Well, I'm ok, this is so new to me, so I am taking it day by day. I really wasn't expecting to be in a relationship let alone now engaged and pregnant. I am truly thankful for everything. I am still finding time taking it all in."* I took her hand and started kissing it, *"I love you and I am here with you."*

"Kaseem, you know, I could have taken a plane or drove up to New York myself, you did not have to come get me." "No way Sin, I had to come get you,

it's a chance for us to have a little road trip and we got hours to talk. Plus, I know you got a lot going on, wedding, baby on the way, business expenses. We family so I figured this is me looking out for you; you have always looked out for me. You introduced me to the woman I am marrying, just think of it as I owe you and I am paying up on it." "I am just going to be so far from Savannah and it is almost time for the baby to be here." "Listen Sincere, your father and I are going to be here with Savannah; you go to your cousin's bachelor party and have fun," my mother said to me while hugging me. *"Don't have too much fun,"* Savannah broke in. *"Come on babe, I'm not even trying to get down like that. I already have one kid on the way; I don't need any more right now,"* I said chuckling. Savannah softly punched me and said, *"I'm serious; now give me and your baby a kiss."* I knelt down and kissed her stomach and said, *"I love you,"* to my unborn child. I stood up and kissed Savannah long and sweet. She put her hands over my head. *"Alright, y'all cut it out, that's why one is on the way now,"* Patricia said laughing. Our families began to laugh along with me and Savannah. I looked Savannah in her eyes and said, *"I love you."* Savannah said, *"I love you too."* My parents hugged each other as Savannah's parents also hugged each other. I looked at Savannah and said, *"I can't go."*

Savannah said, *"No, baby go, I'll be alright." "Now you take care of my baby Kaseem,"* my mother said to Kaseem as she gave him a hug and kiss on the cheek. *"Come on Aunty, you know I will."* I looked at Savannah and said, *"If you need me, call me and I will be back here in no time." "Sin, please I have our parents. Trust and believe I am not having our baby without you here. Time is short but I still have time." "Okay, I love you babe." "I love you too Sin, now go."* Our parents all walked into Savannah's house. I could hear my father say, *"Who's up for a game of Bid Whist?" "That sounds like a plan,"* Travis answered. Both of our mothers said, *"Oh boy here we go,"* and started laughing. Savannah walked up to the Lexus SUV and said, *"Listen Kaseem, you take care of my baby and make sure he behaves." "Come on girl, you know I got you, do not worry, no strippers, just a bunch of dudes chillin'."* Savannah gave Kaseem a 'yea okay' look and said, *"Yea, alright Kaseem, but if I hear any different, I'm coming after you." "Okay."* I came up behind Savannah and hugged her. She turned around and I kissed her. *"Come on man let's go."* I looked in Savannah's eyes and said, *"Baby take care of yourself." "I will,"* Savannah said while holding my hand. I waved to her as she walked back to the house; she blew a kiss at me when she got inside behind the screen door. Kaseem slowly pulled off.

"Man, I miss her already," I said looking out the window. *"Dag you really love her huh?" "Yea, man." "I'm glad to see that you bounced back man. You were a wreck not too long ago." "Yea I know." "So why are you waiting till after she has the baby to marry her?" "I don't want her to be stressed. I mean I want us to plan our perfect wedding and not have to worry about time. Plus, she didn't want to be showing when we got married and come on, you of all people should know the stress that comes with planning a wedding." "Yep, that is exactly what I am going through now Sin." I can only imagine Ka."* I started laughing. My cell phone started ringing, "Never" by Jaheim. *"Na that's my joint let it play,"* Ka yelled as I went to answer it. *"It's the wife man, stop being lazy and download the song for yourself."* *"Hello,"* Savannah said. *"What's up baby? What? You're in labor?"* Kaseem pulled the truck over to the side of the road abruptly and I started laughing. *"Sincere, you are wrong,"* Savannah said. *"Yo Sin don't even play like that, that's not funny." "My bad Kaseem, did you get scared?"* I said laughing while acting concerned. Kaseem started driving again. *"I miss you too baby,"* I said to Savannah. *"I'm gonna kill your husband Savannah,"* Kaseem screamed in

my direction. *"Sincere behave yourself, stop it,"* Savannah said to me. Kaseem started driving again. *"What's up, mama?" "Nothing, just seeing how you were doing and wanted to tell you that I love and miss you." "I love you too mama, I wish I could hold you and kiss you on your forehead. How's my little one?" "Well the baby is up. I wonder if she knows that you are gone, she's been up since you left." "What's all this she talk?" "Oh, did I say she...it could be a he,"* Savannah said with a little giggle. *"Do you know something I don't baby?" "No, I'm going to be just as surprised as you the day the baby is born, Sincere." "Oh okay." "Well I'm not going to hold you up; I'll talk to you later baby." "Ok boo."* We both said, *"I love you"* and hung up. *"Dag, y'all can't be five minutes without each other. I thought me and Ashley were bad. Ay yo Sin, I am not playing Jaheim with another dude in the car." "Are you serious? This is me."* Just then Kaseem's phone started going off, playing "Girlfriend" by Bow Wow and Omarion. *"Yea you are such a thug Kaseem,"* I said sarcastically while laughing. *"Shut up man, it's the Mrs." "What up baby?" "Yea I got him with me, yea hold on."* Kaseem handed me the phone. *"Hello?" "What up Sincere?" "What up girl?" "What's been going on, I heard about the wedding, the baby, you making big moves huh?"*

"Well I'm trying." "I see you making moves marrying this knucklehead over here." Ashley started giggling. *"Yea that's my baby," "He's over here telling me how he's a manly man and a thug." "What? He only has R&B playing in the car, he is not a thug." "Oh really?" "Are you kidding, he tears up when we make love."* I started giggling, trying to hold it back as best as I could, but it came out anyway. *"What? What's so funny?"* Kaseem asked. *"Don't laugh at him Sincere; I think it's cute and romantic,"* Ashley said giggling. *"Oh, I'm not hating,"* I said while laughing. *"Man give me back my phone,"* Kaseem said while snatching his phone back. *'What's up baby? You told him what? Oh come on baby,"* Kaseem said smiling the whole time. *"Yea I love you too beautiful, holla back at me."* Kaseem looked at me. *"Yea you love her,"* I said while grinning. *"Go ahead and throw Jaheim on and play "Never,"* Kaseem said while trying to sound as tough as he could. *"She turned you into a softie,"* I said laughing. *"Oh, shut up Sin, your girl did the same to you." "Yes, I know but I haven't tried to deny it."* As soon as the song came on, we both started bobbing our heads trying not to sing but we would look at each other out of the corners of our eyes to see if we could catch the other person singing the song.

We pulled up in front of my old place. *"Whoa you guys really kept my place up,"* I said admiring the house. I picked up my phone and called Savannah. *'Hey baby." "Sin what's wrong? There's something different about your voice. You sound upset." "Na, boo I'm alright. I just haven't been here in a minute, it caught me by surprise." "Oh, okay baby you sure you alright?" "Yea babe I'm fine, I love you." "I love you too." "How could you lie to her like that Sin?"* Kaseem asked both hurt and concerned. *"I don't want to worry her, what am I supposed to say, it hurts like heck?" "I guess I feel you, but we are here to have a good time, so get it together."*

I slowly got out of the truck and looked at the house. So many memories started coming back, and I just stood there frozen. *"Hey since my room was yours when you lived here you can crash in it if you want. Now come on Sin, and let's get this night started,"* Kaseem said, putting his arm around my neck. Uncle Buba and Aunt Chloe met us at the door. *"Hey how are you doing Sincere?" "Good and you Aunt Chloe?" "Good baby," "How is the little one?"* asked Uncle Buba. *"Growing. Yep we are getting closer to that day."* Uncle Buba started chuckling. I looked around the house. *"Whoa you guys did a great job." "Thank you, Sincere,"* Aunt Chloe answered. I was starting to feel better. *"Ok, you know the party is about to go down in a couple of hours,"* Kaseem said excited. *"Baby we need to get ready, we can't be late for our reservations,"* Uncle Buba said to Aunt Chloe. *"Let's get going sweetie,"* Aunt Chloe answered back.

"Alright boys, let the fun begin," Kaseem said as all the fellas started rolling in. *"Sincere boy what you doing here?"* *"Smokey, what's the deal playa?"* *"It's been a minute baby boy."* *"I know Smoke, I've been trying to get things together,"* *"Yea, I feel ya. I can't even imagine."* *"Smoke I pray you never have to."* Smokey put his hand on my shoulder as he passed by me. I started chuckling as the "crew" walked in. Now this would not be a party without Jaheim, Khalil, Ray and Roscoe. *"What's up fellas?"* *"Sincere what's up man?"* Ray asked. *"Nothing much."* *"How's little mama?"* Jaheim asked. *"She's good."* *"How's our newest little cousin?"* Roscoe asked. We all looked at each other and said *"growing"* and then we started laughing. *"Sincere, out of all the knuckleheads in the world that Savannah could have chosen to be with, I'm glad it's you man, for real from my heart."* *"Thanks Khalil, really."* *"Enough of the sentiments, let's go party fellas, we are supposed to be celebrating, not getting teary-eyed and mushy."* *"See Jaheim, that attitude is why you don't have a shorty now."* *"Whatever man,*

I got plenty of shorties." "Yea, yea that's what they all say," I replied to Jaheim. *"Come on fellas let's go party." "Hey Sin!" "Yea Ray?" "How did that dude Smoke get that name?" "Oh, he was the fastest runner in school, he made records that still have not been broken, and we used to say, 'there he goes leaving them in smoke'."*

All the fellas sat around, ate some wings and had a few drinks. Khalil jumped up and said, *"Ok now it's time for the entertainment."* He made a quick phone call as all the guys started getting excited. Four beautifully shaped women walked through the door. There was one light-skinned African American with hazel eyes and one medium brown-skinned African American with green eyes, one Haitian/Korean with light brown eyes and the last was Columbian with blue eyes. The ladies were definitely hot to death. The Columbian lady came up to me and said, *"You like what you see papi, how would you like it if I was all over you and you were caressing my body?"* I looked at her, took a sip of my drink, took a breath and said, *"You are a very beautiful young lady, but the only woman I want is back home pregnant with my child. One night with you can cost me a lifetime with her, so you can have any other guy you want in this room and be their fantasy woman, but I already have my dream girl and she is waiting at home for me."* (I am not going to lie, you would have thought that was hard to say, but it wasn't at all). The woman just looked at me in shock as if she were never turned down before. I think everyone in the room including me was shocked at what I had just said. She stepped back, looked at me and said, *"You are so sweet, there needs to be more guys like you in the world."* It's true I love Savannah more than life itself and I would not want to disrespect her. Being all over another woman while she is back at home pregnant with my baby, that's just trifling. The ladies started walking into the other room. *"Come on Sin, we won't tell,"* Roscoe said. *"Na, bro, I wouldn't even think to get down like that, I'm engaged to your cousin plus she's back at home pregnant with my baby are you serious?"* Roscoe looked at Ray, Khalil and Jaheim and then went on, *"Yea we would kill you."* At that we all started laughing. *"You gentleman have fun and uh don't do anything I wouldn't do." "That doesn't leave much,"* I heard Khalil say as the guys started heading to the room with the ladies. We all started laughing. Just before going into the room Jaheim turned around and said, *"Go call your sweetheart, we ain't mad at ya."* *"Ok,"* I said getting up and walking over to the stairwell behind the front door. I was sitting there looking out the glass window by the door. *"Hey baby." "Hey Sincere, you having fun?" "Na I'm just chilling."*

"You better not be having too much fun, I know how our cousins and all of your friends are," Savannah said jokingly. I laughed, *"How are you feeling baby?" "I'm okay," "How is the baby?" "We're sitting here missing you." "I miss y'all too baby, I'll be home soon." "Ok boo, I'm gonna go to bed, I'll talk to you later." "Okay, baby sweet dreams, I love you." "I love you too. Hey?" "Yea baby?" "Tell my nasty cousins, I said be careful messing around with them strippers." "Alright." "Oh and Sin?" "Yea babe?" "Don't be messing with them girls either because I will cut you." "You sound so sexy when you make threats baby." "Oh I do?" "Yea." "Alright baby I'll talk to you later." "Goodnight Savannah." "Goodnight Sincere."* The music was bumping and every now and then the fellas would start whooping and hollering so I went upstairs to my old room. I looked around the room I had spent so much time with Cyan in, but now it's Kaseem's so I know him and Ashley have been "blessing" it. I looked around the room and noticed that there was a picture of Cyan and I on the dresser. It was the night we got engaged. The picture was taken at the High Rise. I changed the sheets just in case and then laid on the bed holding the picture on my chest.

I don't remember falling asleep, so I don't know if it was a daydream or not but Cyan walked into the

room in a white mesh jersey. It looked familiar because she would wear it to sleep. It came down to
about her mid-thigh and she always looked amazing
in it especially when she would leave her hair out.
She climbed on me, kissed my lips and then laid her
head on my chest. I could smell her; I could smell
her hair, I could feel her warm soft body. She intertwined her fingers in mine. She looked at me with
those beautiful eyes, smiled at me and said, *"Sincere
it's time to let me go."* Tears started falling down my
face as I said, *"Cyan I can't…. I love you…Why did
you have to go?"* *"Baby, it was my time. You love
Savannah but you are not giving her your all because
you are holding on to me. I want you to be happy and
for you to truly be happy you have to let go. I promised you that you would be fine. I know it is hard to
understand that but please trust me. Sincere you are
my heart and soul but baby you have been holding
onto me for so long you almost missed out on love. I
can stay in your heart forever, I will always be with
you, but you have to let me go."* Cyan softly kissed
me and then laid her head on my chest. It was like
she was breathing me in for the last time. She started
to get up and I tried to hold on to her. As a tear fell
down her cheek, she softly said, *"Sincere…baby you
have to let me go."* Cyan got up and kissed me on my

cheek. *"I never left you Sincere, I love you." "I love you too."* Cyan walked out of the room.

"Come on man, wake up." "What, what? I'm up Ka," I said jumping up out of my sleep clinging onto the picture of Cyan and I. *"You ready to go?" "Huh, what are you talking about Ka?"* I asked while rubbing the sleep out of my eyes. *"I'm taking you back; I know how much you miss Savannah." "Na, you don't have to do that, you've been partying all night and you want to make a trip like that?" "I'm good, don't sweat it." "At least let me jump in the shower man." "Alright but hurry up."*

"So, did you have fun?" I asked while Kaseem and I were getting into the car. *"Yea it was cool, but it just didn't do anything for me man, you know what I am saying Sin?" "Yea man we're getting older and growing up, settling down can do it to you." "Where did you get this picture of Cyan and I?"* I said showing the picture to Kaseem. *"Your mother found it while getting the rest of your things together since you decided to stay in VA. She did not want to open an old wound, so she left it in your room. I kept it because it was the last time I saw you happy." "Ka, before I left, I gave Cyan's parents all of our pictures, I just couldn't deal with it. I hugged them and have not seen them since." "They are doing great, they moved to Hawaii about a year ago. I remember*

your mother introducing them to me, my moms and pops right before they left town. They asked about you before they left. Cyan's mother was hoping that you found love again. Your mom told her that you were still trying to find your way back to love. Hey, you can have that picture of you and Cyan because Savannah has put that smile back on your face. Just make sure I get a family picture." "Definitely Ka. *Yea I remember Cyan's parents telling me that I would be alright and in time I needed to find love again because Cyan would want me to be happy in life."* Just then I got a call on my cell phone. *"Hey baby." "When are you coming home baby? I miss you." "I'll be home tomorrow,"* I said half giggling because I knew I was lying. *"Okay,"* Savannah said in a real sad voice. *"Oh, baby don't sound so sad, I'm coming home right now; you want me to come home?" "Yes....no, stay up there and have fun." "I'll be home before you know it, okay?" "Yea call me later, okay?" "Yea baby I will, I love you." "I love you too." "Later."* We both hung up. *"Oh, Kaseem, run me by the school real quick." "No problem."* The World of Music School and Daycare. I remember when I got this place started. Kaseem and I walked into the school and went into my old office. *"Well, well why does it not surprise me to see you two together?"* *"Hey mama,"* Kaseem said.

"Hey aunty." "You know Sincere before we moved, you two were inseparable, always had to do everything together, now you are all grown up and getting married." "How's business aunty?" "Good, normal as usual." "Kaseem shouldn't you be back at work?" "No mama I took the day off to take Sincere back home." "Oh, that's nice but you need to be working and saving up your money for this wedding." "I know mama." "How's business in Virginia Sincere?" "Good, the school is running fine; I got it going about two months ago. The horse-riding academy is going good too. Savannah's father and I got it started and the first class is about to graduate. We are looking to expand it to run more classes." "Oh, your grandmother would have been so proud to see how well you are doing." "Thank you, aunty." "I've been meaning to ask you, what does Savannah do?" "I never told you guys?" Aunt Chloe and Kaseem both replied, *"No." "Oh, she's a stripper, yeu but she has been having a hard time with it since she's pregnant. Even though the fellas love her belly she can't move like she used to." "You know you are dead wrong,"* Kaseem said laughing. I started laughing. *"You know you are too fresh,"* my Aunt Chloe said. *"What?"* I said innocently. *"The best part was the look on your face, Aunt Chloe." "You know I should beat you, boy," "Aww, Aunt Chlowee, you*

upset with me?" *"Wow, I haven't heard you call me that in a long time, I'm shocked you still remember that."* I called her that up until I was about six and I guess it stuck over time. People would make jokes and call her that all the time especially when they said something to upset her or they were in trouble. *"Savannah owns her own fashion magazine, she started it in New York, then started another company up in North Carolina and just opened up another company in Virginia. She was doing a lot of the day-to-day operations up until recently. Now she only checks in and is on an emergency basis only."* *"Wow, that's nice. Well you boys have a safe trip back, alright baby?"* *"Sure thing mama."* *"Love you aunty, you coming down when the baby is born?"* *"Child I already have my bags packed."*

Kaseem and I headed to the record company. *"Well, well, well if it isn't uncle Buba."* *"Hey boys."* *"Whoa it's weird not seeing you and daddy together, the dynamic duo."* Uncle Buba started chuckling. *"It's no surprise that y'all married women that happened to be sisters either,"* Kaseem stated. *"You know how players do, where do you think you two got it from?"* *"Wow did he really just say that?"* Kaseem turned to me and asked. *"Yea Ka he said it."* *"Hey pop, I need to run down to my office I'll swing by and see you on my way out." "Where are you going?" "To take Sincere home." "Alright."* We were walking down towards Kaseem's office when I saw Alana sitting in front of Ashley's desk talking to her. *"Oh no you have to be kidding me." "Head to the truck and I'll be there in a few Sin." "Hurry up Kaseem…seriously."* As I headed toward the elevator my stomach was in knots. *"Hey baby." "What up girl?" "You had fun at your bachelor party?" "Na, girl, the party was for the guys, not for me." "Yea I bet,"* Ashley said smiling. *"Oh, don't act like you are innocent, how was your party?" "It was fine, I was a good girl." "Where's your cousin, I know he's up here?"* Alana asked Kaseem interrupting Ashley and Kaseem's conversation. *"He's around,"* Kaseem answered. *"Humph, so what hoochie was all up in his face?" "No one, but you are not his girl so what does that matter?" "Whatever, tell my baby I said hi." "Whatever." "Kaseem you're going to be my brother how can you be so mean?" "It's not that I am being mean, it's just he has a girl and a life, you need to respect that and move on with your life." "Humph,"* Alana answered and then added, *"Hey I'll see you two later."* Alana walked away. *"Ashley what's wrong with her?" "Well she loves your cousin and is upset that things did not work out the way she thought it would." "You mean to tell me once Cyan died, Sincere was supposed to go be with her?"* "I guess." *"You gotta be kidding me, sounds like she was waiting for Cyan to die or until Cyan was out of the way."* *"Wait Kaseem I know you are not suggesting...."* Ashley started getting very angry. *"No ma,"* Kaseem said interrupting *"All I am saying is the whole situation is messed up and.... I don't know I'm sorry if you thought I was suggesting...."* Ashley cut Kaseem off by putting her finger on his lips. *"It's alright baby, call me later."* *"Okay baby, I love you."* *"I love you too Kaseem."*

SIX

"Hey baby, wake up." I awoke to see Alana standing by my window. *"I knew you were here,"* Alana said excited. *"What do you want Alana?"* I said with a frown on my face. *"I just wanted to see you baby."* *"I'm not your baby Alana."* *"Alana, will you leave the man alone?"* Kaseem said while walking toward the truck. *"It's about time man,"* I said to Kaseem. *"Well I'm just here to pick up Ashley's car because my car is in the shop; it's not my fault your parking space is next to hers."* *"Well whatever, let the man be."* *"I'll see you later baby,"* Alana said smiling. *"No, you won't, and I am not your baby,"* I said angrily. Alana got into Ashley's car and pulled off. *"I can't stand that chick man, for real."* *"Sin, don't sweat it man."* At that time, my phone rang. *"Hello? Baby? What's wrong?"* *"Nothing boo, how are you?"* *"You sure baby?"* *"Yea I'm cool ma, more importantly, how are you?"* *"I'm good."* *"How is the baby?"* *"Kicking my butt,"* Savannah said giggling. *"Your child misses you; the baby must know you are not here,"* *"Aww, you make me wanna come home."* *"Baby I'm fine I promise I can wait*

*another day." "Okay Boo, I'll see you soon, okay?"
"Yea." "I love you Savannah." "Love you too." We
both said "later" and hung up. "Man, Kaseem I feel
so empty without her next to me." "Yea, I know the
feeling man; well it's time to get you home to your
woman and unborn child." "Let's roll." We were on
our way back to VA, when Kaseem just blurted out
of nowhere, "I can't believe they never found Cyan's
killer." "I know; they just gave me some nonsense
about how they never found my car or had any leads;
I guess eventually they just let it go." "So, you mean
to tell me, if you had the chance to catch the dude
that did it, you wouldn't?" "Of course I would, but
what can I really do? Beat him up? Put him behind
bars for life? Kill him? It wouldn't do anything. Sure,
I would be happy if Cyan were still here because we
would have had a life together, but I guess she had
to die. I just think GOD had a different plan for my
life. I guess things just had to be this way. I still got
engaged and am having a kid. I would rather have
married Savannah first, but there is no reason to fret
over about it now."*

"Hey Alana, did you get everything you needed
done?" "Yea sis thanks for letting me borrow your
car until mine gets out of the shop." "No problem
sis." "Oh my gosh, Sincere looked so good today."
"You saw him, but how?" Ashley asked shocked. "I

went downstairs to get in your car and Sincere was sitting in Kaseem's SUV. Ashley I'll be happy when Sincere and I are finally together. I should be his wife. I should be Mrs. Alana Robinson, yea that's what I'm talking about." "Well, I hate to break it to you sis, but the only one that will ever be able to claim Sincere's name is Savannah." "Well we'll just see about that Ashley, after all, look at what happened with Cyan." "That's wrong Alana, that's not funny, how could you say something like that? Especially when you know Cyan's death has not been solved." "What are you trying to say Ashley that I killed Cyan or had her killed?" "No, I'm not trying to say that, but Alana what you are saying doesn't make you look good either. Why would you even bring something like that up. Please tell me..." "Ashley I can't believe my own sister thinks I'm capable of something like that." Alana stated, interrupting Ashley. *"Alana, you have been after the man for years and then out of nowhere his girl gets killed? Sincere never had problems, so why then?"* *"Someone robbed him for his car, Cyan got killed in the process. Did you forget Sincere got shot too, now why would I let something like that happen to my baby?" "Just forget it Alana I'm sorry I brought it up."*

"Sin what is it about Savannah that does it for you?" "It's just her, everything, her personality, her smile, she's my muse. She gave me my motivation and drive back, I opened up a second school and started a riding academy. With the baby on the way I just got me a brand-new BMW 750LI." "Wow Sin, Savannah really brought you back to us. I'm not happy that Cyan died, but I am happy that you met Savannah…we were really worried about you…the whole family was. It was like you totally shut down. It was kind of scary," "Enough about me Kaseem, what about you, why Ashley?" "The sex yea defi-nitely the sex." At that we both started laughing. *"Na man, on the serious side, I just thought it was a sign from GOD. We kicked it back in the day, didn't see each other for a minute and then we're face to face again. I definitely believe GOD brought us back to-gether, besides that when people say I'm banging my secretary and talk about how I am cheating at least I can say na, my secretary is my wife." "Kaseem?" "Yea man." "You stupid." "Yea I know, all day every day." "Just think about it man, I have access to her 24/7, we can do it in my office, a quickie dur-ing lunch…." "Kaseem,"* I broke in, *"No more, please man, I don't need to hear about you and Ash-ley's sexcapades, please spare me man." "Aww sounds like you're frustrated and have tension Sin."*

"What are you talking about?" "It just sounds like little mama ain't giving you none no more." "Yea, okay I got some right before we left." "How do you do it Sin?" "Very carefully." "Sin you stupid." "I know. Kaseem, it's amazing when the woman you are in love with, you just can't get enough of, your life, your everything, is also pregnant with your child. I have a newfound respect man, because I can't even imagine what it's like to be pregnant, man." "Yea I feel you Sin." "I mean Kaseem, there is just something about Savannah that…it's not that I can't live without her, but I don't want to live without her. I mean when she told me she was pregnant, I was happy…" "Sin, remember how hard our parents emphasized that we should not be getting any girls pregnant, heck not even having sex before we were married?" "Yea, but you know what I know it's because of GOD, our faith and beliefs that we are where we are today. Sure, we slipped up, heck we are partners in crime forever, but now that we are older, we don't do half the things we used to do." "Oh, you know it Sin; we were horrible, I'm glad we matured man." "Well we are here, Sin." "Thanks for looking out for me Kaseem." "Aww come on now, we fam and nothing is going to change that, I never told you this, but I was heartbroken and mad at myself when Cyan got killed. I felt like I let you guys down. I felt

like I should have been there that night to protect y'all and have y'all's back." "Kaseem, it will never be your fault. I guess it was just something that had to happen. You were not meant to be there. What if you lost your life? Do you really think anything would be any better?" "Well...." I cut Kaseem off. *"Kaseem, don't give it another thought. There is nothing you can do about it. What's done is done. Don't stop living your life over something you had no control of; I will never hold you responsible for that. I never cared about the car. I didn't care that the dude took it, what got me was he shot at us while our backs were turned like a coward. I feel like I lost my girl over a car. She didn't have to die man, but I guess it was just her time. Life is funny and the way things go are just crazy, but I guess life is not meant to be understood, it's just meant to be lived. If we spent all our time trying to understand why certain things happen in life, we will just let it pass us by."* I looked at the picture of me and Cyan and ran my finger over her face. *"I guess you are right Sin."*

"Baby what you doing?" "Hey you, I'm just sitting here in the rocking chair talking to our mothers." "What would you say if I was sitting right outside?" "I would say shut up, stop lying and don't play with my emotions." "Oh okay, I was just wondering." Just then I heard my mother say, *"Hey that*

looks like Kaseem's truck out there." "Don't play with me Sincere are you really outside?" "I don't know you just may have to come and see." "Don't make me get up and walk all the way to the door for no reason." Just then I heard Savannah's mother say, *"Veronica that does look like his truck." "Hey Marques, is that Kaseem and Sincere outside?"* Patricia asked in the direction of me and Savannah's fathers. Marques and Travis walked to the door. Marques said, *"It better be them, because whoever it is, is disturbing me and Travis' card game."* Patricia said, *"You, Travis, and your card games."* Travis replied, *"What? You and Veronica sit and talk all day long, so Marques and I have to find something to do." "If it's not cards, it's football,"* Veronica said. *"Hey fellas,"* my father said excited while Kaseem and I were getting out of the truck. *"Hey daddy, what's up?" "Nothing, I wish you had let us know you were on your way back." "What and ruin the surprise?" "How was the trip boys?"* Travis asked. *"Not bad at all, we made good timing, traffic wasn't bad at all,"* I answered. *"You know I had to get Sincere home to both of his babies,"* Kaseem said with a laugh. *"Hey Sugar,"* my mother said cheerfully. *"Hey mama." How are you feeling?" "A little sleepy, but that's all." "So come on in and get something to eat and then go take yourself a nap." "I know you boys are hungry,"* Patricia stated. *"You know we are, Mrs. Williams,"* Kaseem agreed. Where is she is all I kept thinking to myself and then she appeared leaning up against the door in a blue sun dress. It was like seeing her again for the first time; a tear almost came to my eye. I pushed my back off the truck and started walking to the house. *"Hey girl,"* I said giving Savannah a hug and kiss on the cheek. *"Hey yourself,"* Savannah said back while holding me. I let her go just a little so I could look into her eyes. *"Baby I love you more than life itself. I missed you so much and that's why I just had to get home to you, I just need you with me." "Baby you alright? Where is all of this coming from?"* I hugged her again and she held me. I softly kissed Savannah on the forehead and then whispered, *"Baby I love you so much and not being here with you made me realize that we definitely need to be together for the rest of our lives. I don't ever want to live without you."* Savannah kissed me on the cheek and whispered, *"I love you too baby."*

My dad grabbed my bag and started in the house. Patricia and Veronica started fixing plates of fried chicken, collard greens, yams, potato salad, and cornbread. After eating, Savannah sat in the rocking chair and I knelt on the floor and had my head in her lap. *"Sincere," "Yea baby?" "The baby is asleep come sit down with me for a sec." Alright."* We walked over to the couch and Savannah laid on her back with her head in my lap. *"Well the baby is due soon." "Yea, I know." "I'm packed and ready to go, we have the money, we have a place to stay, I just wish we were married already." "I know baby, well how long do you want to wait until after the baby is born to get married?" "I was thinking about August. The baby will be three months old and I know I will definitely be healed up by then and hopefully lose some of this weight. I mean I do little workouts and I haven't gained much weight so it's basically all baby." "So, you are saying you should be back to normal in no time huh?" "Yep." "You're ready to go to sleep?"* I asked Savannah. *"Yea boo."* We went to the bedroom and got in the bed. *"I love you baby,"* Savannah whispered. *"I love you too sweetheart, goodnight,"* I whispered back. *"Baby I'm glad you are home; I was a little worried because I was like what if the baby decides to come early? Now that you are home, everything is good, goodnight."* After Savannah fell asleep, I sat up in bed, just watching her and started stroking her hair. *"Baby, why are you still up?"* my mother asked after softly knocking and then opening the door. *"Ever since I've been staying here with her, I always get up after she falls asleep; I just sit here and watch her." "That is so sweet,"* Patricia said walking through the door after my mother. *"What are y'all still doing up?"* *"Well we were having a cup of tea and talking before me and your father left to go across the street."* *"Let me guess they are playing cards, aren't they?"* *"You know it,"* my mother said. *"They can play all night you know,"* Patricia added. *"Yea tell me about it,"* I answered shaking my head while chuckling. *"Alright baby get some rest, we'll see you later."* *"Alright mama. Love ya mama."* *"Love you too baby."* My mother walked out of the room. *"You really love my daughter huh?"* *"Yes ma'am."* I looked down at Savannah, placed my hand on her head and stroked her hair, looked back up at Patricia and added, *"With everything that I am."* Patricia smiled shaking her head in approval and walked out after saying, *"Goodnight my son."* I quickly said, *"goodnight mama,"* and heard Patricia start giggling. Savannah opened up her eyes and looked at me as I was caressing her head. She smiled, placed her hand on the back of my neck and asked, *"Baby, what's wrong?"* *"Nothing boo."* *"You sure?"* I gave her a kiss on the forehead and told her *"yea."* *"Baby you need some rest, go to sleep."* *"Savannah you sound just like our mothers."* Savannah started giggling. *"Sincere do you ever get scared?"* *"Of what babe?"* *"You know, becoming a parent?"* *"Na, not really. I think we will be great parents. We were raised by great parents and I hope that we learned from them and use what we learned to teach our child." "Yea, I just wonder if I am going to be a good mother." "Baby, you are going to be a great mother." "You think?" "I know." "Well I think you are going to be a great father." "Well, thank you baby." "You're welcome sweetheart."*

   "Alright you two, time for a game of Spades," Travis said while knocking on the door. *"Oh daddy you have to be kidding me." "No, baby right after we eat breakfast the game is on." "Daddy!" "What? It's a chance for me and your mother to spend time with you and Sincere." "I know but daddy we just went to sleep about three hours ago." "Okay sweetheart we'll let you sleep a little longer, but breakfast will be ready soon." "Okay daddy." "Love you sweetheart." "Love you too daddy."* Travis walked out of the room. *"I cannot believe that man." "Oh baby, he's not too bad. He wants to spend time with us, look at it like this - you are your father's baby. Well his baby is about to be married and have a family of her own. He may feel like he's losing you, so cut him a little slack. He's dealing with it the best way he knows how." "I guess you are right baby. Well it's time to get up anyway Sincere." "Why baby?" "Because the baby is up and the baby is not going to let me get any more sleep."*

"Well, good morning sunshine." "Good morning mama." "How is my grandbaby?" "Up and active." Patricia smiled. *"Aww poor Sincere, you look so tired baby, go back and get you some sleep baby." "Na, I'm alright mama, it's time for me to get up anyway." "No, I don't want to hear it, go get back in the bed." "Mama." "What did I say?"* Patricia put her hands on her hip and gave me a "don't make me repeat myself" look. *"Yes ma'am I'm going." "That's right." "Mama, Sincere is a grown man; you can't make him go back to bed." "Sincere is my son and he needs his rest, the boy doesn't sleep because he stays up all night watching you, but now that we are up, he can sleep. Just look at him, poor baby fell asleep at the table." "Baby,"* Savannah said while tapping me. *"Come on baby let me get you back in the bed."* I got up and started back to the room. Savannah came up behind me and hugged me. I started giggling, *"What are you doing baby?" "Nothing."* I let Savannah pass me and held her by the waist. *"Are you thinking what I'm thinking?" "No, are you kidding me Sincere, with my parents up and walking around?"* I kissed Savannah on the back of her neck. *"Baby stop,"* Savannah said softly with sex in her voice. *"Baby you look so good, I gotta have you." "Oh yeah I'm waddling here."* I started laughing. Savannah reached back and lightly hit me in my head

and said jokingly, *"Don't laugh at me, only I can laugh at my fat jokes, you're not allowed."*

"Ay Sin, it's time for me to get home to my little lady." "Cool deal fam, thanks for everything." "No problem fam." I really do not like to see my cousin leave. Like our fathers we are inseparable, we used to hang tight 24/7, but I guess we have to also live our own lives. I watched my cousin pull off and I walked into Big Mama's house. Man, I feel like I haven't been here in like forever. The more Savannah came closer to her due date the less I stayed at Big Mama's house. I looked at the Kawasaki Ninja ZX-14R that Kaseem left me and remembered how Savannah refused to ride on it and used to always tell me to get rid of it. The moment she got pregnant all she would tell me was, *"You know that bike has got to go, you have a baby on the way and your child needs their father."* I just laughed to myself and said, *"You know what she's right."* If she heard that I would never hear the end of it.

"If I could tell you how you set my heart on fire. You're my heart, my love my desire. There's no one else in the world that can do the things that you do. Holding me, caressing me, kissing me, loving me, touching me, making love to me, oh I love the way our bodies move. I melt into you; you melt into me, no one in between, baby we are meant to be. The way

our bodies intertwine, we forget about the time, oh baby you're making me wet, we're starting to sweat, you got me bent, I'm drunk off your love, flying free like a dove. Baby I love the way you're turning me on. Our love runs deep, I find myself trying to figure out exactly where our hearts meet. Every night I watch you sleep, lay my hand on your chest just to feel your heartbeat. I can't believe this, not only am I about to be your wife; I'm also having your baby. I can't thank you enough for letting me have the honor and pleasure of being your lady." Savannah closed her book and put it on her night table along with the pen. She sat and rubbed her stomach while watching me sleep with a smile on her face.

"Do you really think they are ready Marques?" "Well Veronica it's too late to turn back now." "I know, but I am still worried." Don't be worried, we raised Sincere right, they both know what they are getting into, they will be just fine." "Yea, you're right," Veronica kissed Marques, turned over and went to sleep.

"Oh Travis, what are our babies going to do? "They'll be fine Patricia, it's not like we're turning our backs on them. We'll be here for support; but at the same time Sincere must be a man and take care of his family. I just can't believe my little girl is having a baby, Tricia." "I know Travis but hey, they own

their own businesses, they're educated, they have an amazing supportive family, they are really set for life." "I know sweetheart." "Savannah is a grown woman and made a decision, as her parents we have to step back and let her live her life." "I never thought she would grow up so quickly, Patricia where did the time go?" "I don't know Travis; all I know is that I'm not ready to be a grandmother." "You? Ha I am nowhere near the age of being a grandfather, I just turned 55." Oh, like I am really old enough, 57 is not that much older Travis." "I know but you're still older," Travis said in a taunting voice. *"Whatever,"* Patricia said hitting Travis lightly and laughing, *"Good night, baby,"* Travis said. *"Good night sweetie,"* Patricia answered back. *"I love you,"* Travis added. *"You sure? I'm old remember, you said I am an old woman." "Yea but…." "Watch what you say Travis, watch your mouth,"* Patricia cut in. *"But,"* Travis started again. *"I'm not playing with you Travis, you are gonna say something that is going to get you in trouble,"* Patricia said laughing. *"Who me? I would never do something like that,"* Travis said innocently. *"Um-hum."* Patricia turned over and Travis put his arm around Patricia, kissed her on the cheek and they both fell asleep.

The next morning

"Hey Sincere let me talk to you for a second," Travis said. *"What up pop?"* I asked concerned. *"Sincere I know about Cyan,"* Travis stated hesitantly. I just looked in astonishment as I slowly started sitting down on the couch. Travis continued. *"It was a cold case I was working and today I received a phone call about someone calling into Crime Stoppers. An anonymous tip was given about Cyan's murder. The caller gave a description of the person and a name. I had the department send me the file and I remembered where I saw your face, it was in the file."* *"Pop what are you trying to tell me?"* I asked. *"Sincere, they found him not too far away from here."* *"Are you telling me they have Cyan's killer?"* *"That is exactly what I am saying, son."* *"I want to see him,"* I said jumping up. *"Wait son."* *"I want to look in the face of her killer."* *"Look all I can tell you is he is cooperating, and he said there is someone else involved and that...that,"* *"That what pop?"* *"That it's your fault why Cyan is dead."* *"Huh? Are you serious?"* *"I have to take you down to the station for questioning."* *"Pop, you have to be kidding me."* *"I wish I was son, I wish I was."* Travis escorted me outside. We both got into Travis' Cadillac Escalade and headed down to the station.

Upon arrival at the station, Travis talked to the officer behind the desk. A man came and sat down next to me. *"I am detective McMillan; I am working with the New York's Sheriff's Office Cold Case Department that is why I contacted Mr. Williams since he was the last person to work the case. I am following up on a lead from a homicide case that I am sure you are familiar with. Do you know why you are here?"* *"It's bogus, I had nothing to do with my fiancée's death, I loved her more than life itself, I would have died for her."* *"Really? Well come with me and we will discuss it."* I walked with the detective to the back to a little room, with a one-way mirror. I inched back horrified and gasped. *"Bryan?"* Travis put his arm around me. *"What was that son?"* Detective McMillan looked at me and asked, *"Do you know him?"* *"Yea, that's Alana and Ashley's cousin, I have seen him a couple of times."* *"Why would he...Alana."* *"What Sincere?"* Travis asked, horrified. *"Detective what is he doing down here?"* I asked him fearfully. *"He says he's hanging out with his cousin; they took a road trip."* *"We got a call to respond to a suspicious vehicle in the area of your house. Upon running the plates, it came back to your stolen BMW, the one from the night of the crime. How it slipped through the cracks up until now is beyond me. We took this young man into custody; however, he is the only person we have. We do not know where or who his cousin is."* "Pop, someone get to Savannah now,*"* I ordered. *"What's wrong Sincere?"* Travis asked with a lump in his throat. *"They are not hanging out, it's another hit. Alana wants Savannah dead."* Travis' heart dropped. Detective McMillan asked, *"What are you talking about?"* *"Alana must have had him kill my fiancée Cyan and use my car as a cover up and now she wants Savannah out of the way. She has wanted me since high school and now she is trying to do anything to make that happen!"* I exclaimed. *"Someone get to my Savannah; she could be in a lot of trouble."* Travis ran out of the door to get to his SUV. *"Stay here detective I'll handle this,"* I said in pure anger. I walked out of the room and entered the room where Bryan was sitting. *"What up Sincere? Sorry we had to meet again under these circumstances,"* Bryan said upon seeing me. *"Why?"* I asked. *"Because you broke my cousin's heart."* *"Cyan was innocent and had nothing to do with it."* *"My cousin wants you and I believed in making her happy, I say believed because she turned me in. Alana said I needed to pay for you getting shot in the process. She switched the plates on my car and turned me in,"* Bryan said with a hurt look on his face. *"Is she with you?"* *"Na, she is probably with your wifey as we speak, nothing is going to stop her Sincere, and she ordered the hit on Cyan. Once she found out about Savannah, Alana wanted her dealt with…if you know what I mean."* "If Savannah gets hurt everyone who played a part will pay." I stormed out of the room and Detective McMillan ordered me a police escort. Detective McMillan got the full confession that he needed.

I frantically tried to call Savannah with no success. I started panicking. *"Hey Sincere stay calm she…."* *"Don't make any promises Pop,"* I said to Travis. *"What is the status?"* *"My wife is at your parent's house. She said Savannah was right behind her and Savannah turned around to get something and said she would meet my wife at your house."* I started dialing numbers; the phone rang. *"Sincere what's up?"* Jaheim answered. *"Jaheim, you, Khalil Ray, and Roscoe need to go to my house now."* *"Sin, what's up?"* *"Jaheim just trust me; I need you and the fellas in place like yesterday."* *"Sin, we are on it."* *"Thanks man."* Sincere, what are you doing?" Travis asked. *"I'm taking care of my family,"* I answered back. Travis threw me a bag and I hopped in the unmarked cruiser with the officer escorting me to the house. The officer drove me a couple of blocks away from the house and let me out, *"We have snipers in place and perimeters set up at both houses.*

Alana is refusing to speak to anyone. Your parents and Savannah's mother are at your house." "Let me go in Officer, that is what Alana wants and that is the only way you will get anything." "This is dangerous, and we would normally never do anything like this, but it looks like you are all we have left, good luck." "Thanks Officer."

I slowly walked up to the house and entered the front door. I walked into the living room and there was Savannah sitting on the couch with tears flowing from her eyes. I looked over at the reclining chair in the corner and said, *"Okay, Alana enough is enough." "Oh, really Sincere? I am in control now."* She pulled out her two-toned Sig Sauer 9mm P239 handgun and said, *"Nice of you to join the party, now sit down."* I sat down next to Savannah, put my arm around her and whispered, *"I will get you and the baby out of this." "Hmmm let's see what do I feel like doing? Should Savannah and the baby go? Wow Sincere you would lose your lady once again, but this time you would lose a baby too." "What does my un-born baby have to do with this? Savannah and the baby did nothing to you; Cyan did not do anything to you either. What's your problem?" "Cyan was in the way; she kept us apart. Savannah is in the way in the same manner. It's really not her fault, it's yours be-cause you started a relationship. You losing your baby is just so you can know how I felt when I lost mine." "What?" I asked with a weird look on my face. "Yes, Sincere I was pregnant by you." "What?" I said again in shock. "When you dumped me to run back to Cyan, I found out I was pregnant. You didn't care and because I was so upset and stressed out, I had a miscarriage." "Why didn't you say anything Alana?" "Like you would have cared? You ran to be with your precious Cyan, you wouldn't even give me a chance. Every time I tried to tell you, either Cyan was there or you would brush me off. The day me and Cyan almost had the big fight was because she heard me talking to Ashley in the hallway after class. Ashley told me not to say anything, she told me not to ever repeat out it loud until we got everything figured out. Your precious Cyan heard me say that I was pregnant by you and she could not stand it. She decided to confront me in hopes that I would shut up and never say a word about it. You came and picked Cyan up to prevent us from fighting. You clearly chose Cyan over me. You chose Cyan over your unborn child." "I never knew, Alana." I figured Cyan never told you and that is why she kept me away from you. "why didn't Ashley tell me, she knew this whole time." I made Ashley promise never to speak of it." "Sincere, I did the only thing left to do to get next to you; I got rid of Cyan. I told my cousin Bryan to take her out. We followed you as you were driving around and when you were at the red light, I told him to go for it. The idiot was not supposed to shoot you in the process and that is why I turned him in." "Alana, it did not have to be that way, you did not have to kill Cyan." "Yes, I did and now I need to kill Savannah and the baby, to make things right. We are supposed to be together." "No, you know what, I have caused all of this pain; you need to take me out." "Sincere what are you saying, what are you doing?"* Savannah asked me, gripping my hand. I let Savannah's hand go and walked up to Alana while she pointed the gun at me. *"Sincere sit down, don't make me do this." "Alana no more, you will hurt no more people, I hurt you, I deserve to pay." "Sincere no,"* Savannah started crying. Tears started falling from Alana's eyes as I walked straight into the gun and had it pointed in my stomach. *"Alana I am sorry, and I will never hurt you again."* I grabbed the gun and forced her to pull the trigger. The gun went off, I backed up a little, looked at Alana, stumbled back to Savannah's feet, fell by her side, put my head in her lap, and exhaled. Alana stood in shock. Savannah started saying, *"Oh no, baby, baby wake up, please don't die on me."* Alana looked at me in shock as the tears started flowing from her eyes. She started to put the gun to her head, and another gun went off. Travis had managed to sneak into the house and shoot Alana in her shoulder. Multiple officers immediately stormed into the house to take Alana into custody. *"No kill me, kill me now,"* Alana started screaming. Travis stood over my body as Savannah was holding me and shaking me trying to desperately wake me up. *"Sincere, it's over we got everything we needed."* Travis said while standing over me. *"Savannah, I know I said I would die for you and take a bullet but that hurt so badly we may have to figure out another way."* I said to Savannah while opening my eyes. *"You're alive? You let me think she killed you? I am so mad at you!"* Savannah screamed at me. *"I had to protect you and the baby; I did what it took even if that meant dying for the two of you." "Daddy you knew about this?" "Sincere said he was going to protect you and the baby; I just simply gave him a vest to put on."* I slowly pulled up my shirt in pain to reveal the bullet proof vest that Travis had given me; it also revealed the wiretap I was wearing. *"You're alive,"* Alana said. *"Oh Sincere..."* Alana started. *"Gentlemen take her away please,"* Travis said. After the police were done doing everything they needed to do, they let everyone into the house: my parents, Savannah's mother, Jaheim, Khalil, Roscoe and Ray. I took Savannah towards the front door and we sat in the open doorway, *"Can you forgive me babe?"* *"I just can't believe that you would let me think you were dead."* *"I had to do it so Alana would not kill you or the baby."* *"You did a good thing; I am not really mad. I just thought I lost you and that was it, you were gone and never coming back. I saw when Cyan died in your arms."* *"I'm sorry baby; I didn't want to put you through that."* *"It's okay babe, it's just ……."* Savannah grew quiet. *"Babe you okay?"* *"Umm I don't know, I think…owwww that doesn't feel good."* I screamed into the house, *"Let's go!"* I physically picked Savannah up and put her in the car and was on the way to the hospital as our families were starting to leave the house. I don't know how it happened but it's like I blinked, and we were at the hospital.

I remember the nurses putting Savannah in a wheelchair but while they were checking her out, they looked at each other, whispered to each other and then had a stretcher brought out to them. They told me I couldn't go into the room with her and it was best that I wait with the family. I sat in the waiting room pacing back and forth wondering if Savannah and the baby were okay. *"Sincere you have to try to calm down,"* my mother said. *"I can't mama, I don't know what to do. Savannah is in there and I can't be by her side,"* I answered back. *"Son it's okay; breathe and try to relax a little. I know it's *easier said than done but I need you to try, you are no good to Savannah and the baby if you pass out or if you can't keep it together for them,"* my father said to me. *"What's going on with our baby Travis?"* Patricia asked her husband. *"I am sure she is fine honey, have faith, I am sure she is fine."* Travis answered his wife while pulling her close. The doctor came out with his head held down and shaking his head. All I could think to myself was no, not again. *"Doc, you gotta tell me something, what is going on?"* *"We did all that we could, it took a lot of work. The baby is fine, you have a baby girl, but your wife lost a lot of blood, she had some tearing and we had to do a lot of repair work. We almost lost her a couple of times. Right now, it seems like we have stopped all the bleeding and she is stable but even that is kind of shaky right now. We will have to watch her closely."* *"Can we go see her?"* *"Well because of what is going on, only one of you can see her."* We all looked at each other; Travis and Patricia looked at each other and nodded in agreement. *"Sincere it should be you, go to Savannah."* *"You sure?"* I asked, looking at the both of them. *"Yes son, we are,"* Patricia said taking my hand. I looked around the room and followed the doctor to her room. The doctor turned around and said to everyone else, *"The nurse will be in soon to take you to see your newest family member.*" He smiled and nodded. The doctor led me to Savannah's room and opened the door.

Savannah was hooked up to a bunch of machines; I was not ready to see her like this. I tried to hold it together, but I could feel the tears welling up in my eyes. I walked over to her and sat down next to her bed. She had IVs in her, a breathing tube, a heart monitor, and there other machines present but at the time I did not care, my baby was laying in this bed and there was a possibility that she would never wake up again, never see our baby girl. I just did not know how to handle that. At the thought of being a single dad and raising our baby without Savannah I said, *"Baby, you are going to be fine, you are too strong to give up. You have a beautiful baby girl waiting for you; we still have a wedding to finish planning; you have to meet me at the altar. There is no way you can leave me. I lost Cyan and I can't lose you. My heart just can't take it baby."* *"Do you want to see your daughter?"* The doctor said poking his head in the door. *"We will see our daughter together and name her together."* *"I don't know if that is a good idea given the circumstances."* *"Doc, I have a faith that you would not believe, faith that I did not even know I had within me. Savannah will wake up; we will see our daughter together and we will name her together. Just have faith Doc, just have faith."* I put my hand underneath Savannah's hand. *"Babe you have to get up, our daughter needs a name."* I sat back in the chair. Travis walked into the room and said, *"Sincere go home and get some rest,"* without taking my eyes off Savannah I said, *"Pop, I can't leave her, you know if it were me in this bed she would tell you the same thing, she would tell you that she can't leave my side. I do not want her to wake up and I am not here." "You should at least go see your daughter." "I can't do it without Savannah it just wouldn't feel right, it's just not fair."*

"Marques, Veronica, you have to tell Sincere something he is refusing to leave Savannah's side," Travis said as he entered the nursery area where Marques, Veronica, and Patricia were all standing. *"Ahh, so you met Sincere's stubborn side; he gets that from Veronica,"* Marques said with a chuckle. *"Once he has his mind set on something he won't budge until it is completed." "I am not that bad Marques,"* Veronica said lightly hitting Marques in the stomach. *"I am sure he will be fine Travis. He loves our daughter. If it was any of us in their place, we would all be doing the same thing as Sincere,"* Patricia said to Travis. *"You are right honey."*

"Sincere baby, you have to see her, she looks just like you." "Mama I can't." "Sincere she needs you, take your daughter." My mother put her in my arms;

she was the cutest little thing. A cute little light skin baby with gray eyes. She definitely had Savannah's dimples. She grabbed my finger. *"Hey baby, I'm so glad you are here."* I kissed her on the cheek. *"Savannah, she is here to see you, wake up baby, say hello to our daughter."* *"Mama, what am I going to do?* *"Just keep believing baby, she is going to wake up, you are going to be a family. Baby you do need to get some rest."* *"I can't mama, not until Savannah wakes up."* *"But Sincere...."* My mother started. *"Have faith and keep believing, remember mama?"* *"Yes, that's right baby."*

"You wanna hear a song I sing to your mother? Okay here it goes," I started singing "You Send Me" by Sam Cooke while feeding the baby a bottle. *"You know you are going to spoil her,"* I heard a whisper over my shoulder. I stopped and smiled. *"It's about time, how long were you going to make me wait? I missed you."* *"I missed you too,"* Savannah whispered. The doctor came in to check on Savannah. *"Wow, you're up."* *"I couldn't let him have all the fun,"* Savannah said to the doctor while nodding her head towards me. The doctor moved Savannah's bed up to check her out. *"How are you feeling?"* *"Sore, but I think I will be okay, why is my throat so sore?"* *"We had you on a breathing tube; we took it out about 5:00 this morning when we saw that you were*

breathing on your own fully. Being sore is normal, you went through a lot." "Bring her here Sincere. It's okay, right doctor?" "If you feel you are strong enough, go for it. I didn't expect to see you up. I have faith, I just must give the medical facts; however, I have a newfound faith after seeing Sincere and your family. Sincere was adamant on staying by your side until you woke up even after giving him all the facts. Well I am done here. I will let your family know what is going on and you enjoy your time with your daugh-ter." Savannah smiled, *"Thanks Doc."* I placed the baby in Savannah's arms. *"Sincere, she is so beauti-ful, she looks just like you." "She has your eyes and your dimples Savannah."* Savannah gave the baby a kiss on the cheek and said, *"Hi baby." "What did we name her Sincere?" "That is something for us to de-cide together, so let's get to it."* After throwing out a couple of names we decided on Serenity. *"That's a beautiful name, Serenity it is,"* Savannah said proudly. At that moment both of our parents entered the room. After I kissed Savannah on the forehead, we told them we named the baby Serenity. They all thought Serenity was a beautiful name.

The court date for Alana had finally come. There were numerous testimonies including myself, Savan-nah, the officers, etc. Even after all of that, Alana's claim of insanity based on the miscarriage was taken into consideration and she was ordered to undergo a psych evaluation before they determined her sentence. Bryan (Alana and Ashley's cousin) was sentenced based on at least six charges to 78 years in prison. For cooperating with the police, he avoided getting a life sentence.

The big day for Kaseem and Ashley arrived. It was a beautiful day in New York. The wedding party was hanging out in a little room and me being who I am started taking bets that Kaseem would cry at the altar. Of course, the ladies said, *"Awww don't do that to him, that's not right Sincere,"* and the fellas said, *"I'm in, how much you want on it?"* After placing the bets, I joined Kaseem. *"You ready?"* I said to Kaseem as I was waiting in the pastor's office. *"Of course I am. Are you ready Sin?"* *"Of course. I was born to be your best man."* *"Hey, thank Savannah for filling in for...you know."* *"She is feeling a little awkward, but she said she wanted you and Ashley's day to be perfect."* *"I'm glad Ashley was so understanding, I was shocked when she asked Savannah to be in the wedding."* *"She felt it was the least she could do Sin, granted what Alana put you, Savannah, and the family through."* *"It's cool, we are just thankful to be here and have Alana far away from us."* *"Ok, gentleman it's time,"* Pastor Wyatt stated when he entered the room. Kaseem and I took our places in the front of the church. Ashley's parents came in, Ashley's father walked her mother to her seat and then went back out, Uncle Buba and Aunt Chloe followed and went to their seats. The wedding party entered the church and took their places in front of the altar. Watching Savannah walk down the aisle made my heart melt. *"This will be you in a month,"* Kaseem leaned over and whispered in my ear. Savannah looked so beautiful; you would not know she had a baby five months ago if she hadn't said anything. Savannah locked eyes with me, smiled and started blushing. I mouthed, *"I love you,"* to Savannah and she mouthed *"I loved you too."* I felt tears starting to come to my eyes, but I quickly played it off like something flew in my eye. I wiped away the tears before anybody caught on to what was going on. The congregation stood up and the doors of the church opened. Ashley was standing in the doorway with her father. Ashley looked beautiful. I looked over at Kaseem who was trying to keep his composure but was so anxious to see his bride. The music started and Ashley's father started to escort her down the aisle. I saw the moment Kaseem caught a glimpse of Ashley, he exhaled and then had a big grin on his face. Ashley got to the altar and after her parents gave her away, Kaseem took Ashley by the hand. The waterworks began just like I knew it. I looked over at the guys in the wedding party and gave them a "pay up" smile and nod. Ashley wiped away Kaseem's tears and I tried my hardest not to laugh. Kaseem tried to keep it together but the tears kept rolling down his face. Wow Kaseem is really in love, I never thought it could happen. I wonder if everyone says the same about me? It was finally time for Kaseem and Ashley to kiss. Kaseem placed Ashley's veil towards the back of her head but he was so excited about kissing her that he didn't get the veil all the way back so a piece of it was sticking on the top of Ashley's hair. Kaseem kissed Ashley and as they finished, Savannah fixed the veil. The pastor announced Mr. and Mrs. Kaseem Robinson, and everyone applauded. After the pictures at the church it was on to the reception hall. The ride over to the reception was fun because of course me and Savannah got to ride in the same car. I whispered in her ear, *"Hey you want to make another baby tonight?"* *"Sincere you are so silly, no we just had Serenity five months ago, you have to give me more time and not without a wedding ring on my finger,"* Savannah whispered back. *"Ok, baby what about our wedding night?"* I whispered *"Sincere, I am not playing with you, do not try to get me pregnant on our wedding night, are you plotting and planning something?"* Savannah whispered back. *"Will you two get a room?"* Khalil said to me and Savannah. *"Hold on wait a second the last time you two did that, Serenity was the result, you two are going in time out - in different rooms,"* Jaheim said following Khalil's statement. Everyone in the limo started laughing. I gave Savannah a real innocent look and said, *"Me, plot, baby?......Never." "Yea right Sincere, I'm not playing with you,"* Savannah softly tapped me in the stomach and started giggling. We arrived at the reception hall.

The reception hall was beautiful. There were crystal chandeliers all around and the reception room had a nice fireplace. After the parents, wedding party and Mr. and Mrs. Kaseem Robinson were announced it was time to party. Everyone had a really good time. We danced the night away. *"You look beautiful baby." "Aww thank you Sincere, you are so sweet, I am glad I have a man like you in my life." "Actually, Savannah you make me a better man, you are my partner, we do this thing called life together." "Yep baby we're in this together, forever and always." "Look at them Sincere."* Savannah said looking in the direction of Kaseem and Ashley. *"They are so happy; they really love each other."* Savannah added. *"They sure do,"* I answered while watching Kaseem and Ashley smile and laugh as they danced.

"You ready?" I asked Savannah. *"Definitely"* Savannah answered back. I leaned down and gave Savannah a soft passionate kiss and then leaned my head against hers as we continued to slow dance.

The family had come to VA for the big wedding. The day was finally drawing near, the day me and Savannah get married. *"Well tomorrow I will be Mrs. Sincere Robinson, are you ready?"* Savannah asked me while we were sitting on the swing chair outside. *"I was ready a long time ago baby,"* I answered back. *"Okay you two, it's a big day tomorrow and no more hanging out until the wedding; besides, we have plans for the both of you,"* Patricia came outside saying. There was a big family dinner. After the dinner of course all of the ladies stayed at Savannah's house and all of the guys stayed at my house. All of the ladies that were married talked about their wedding day and gave Savannah gifts. The guys well what else would we do? We played cards and talked about the days of being a bachelor. It was a joining of two families for a good time.

"Today is the day, it's been a long time coming but it's here," I said to myself as I was getting dressed in the mirror. *"You ready?"* my father said while walking into the room. Two Cadillac limos pulled up. We started pouring into the limos. My parents in one and the crew in mine: Jaheim, Kaseem,

Khalil, Ray and Roscoe. As we were leaving, Savannah's Jaguar limo and another Cadillac limo was pulling up in front of Savannah's house. Well, next stop Ebenezer Baptist Church. We got to the church as everyone was starting to settle into their seats. I got out of the car in my white tuxedo, white ascot tie, white cummerbund, white shoes, white derby hat, white cane, and of course I had the white gloves hanging out of my pocket. The guys were in black tuxedos with blue bowties and cummerbunds. I met with Pastor Wright who was presiding over the wedding. *"Hey Sincere, you ready?" "Of course, pastor, just waiting on the bride." "Well it's her day and you know they are fashionably late on the wedding day." "As long as she gets here, I am good to go, Pastor."* We started laughing. Just then the pastor's wife walks in and says, *"The girls' car just pulled up."* I got really nervous. Wow it's actually time. The organist got in place and started playing music while Kaseem and I took our places in the front of the church. Savannah's grandmother was escorted in. Our mothers were then escorted in. Savannah's father escorted Savannah's mother in to her seat and then went back out, then my father escorted my mother in. Each lady of the wedding party was escorted in by one of the guys in the wedding party. The girls were wearing different shades of blue and the guy's ties and cummerbunds matched the girl's dress that they were escorting. The ring bearer came in. Ashley was the matron of honor and she came in followed by the carpet rollers and the flower girls. The church stood up and faced the doors. I heard gasps and heard many women saying how beautiful Savannah looked. I could not see her. I tried to catch a glimpse, but everyone was in my way. I finally caught a glimpse of her. She looked amazing. She was in her white wedding gown with a diamond tiara and she was wearing the diamond necklace and bracelet I bought and had delivered to her that morning. She made her way down the aisle escorted by her father and all I could think to myself was, that's my angel. Savannah's mother was holding Serenity. As Savannah passed her, I saw Savannah's mother say, *"You see how beautiful your mommy is?"* Savannah got to the altar and all we could do is stare and smile at each other. *"Who gives this woman away?"* the pastor asked. *"I and her mother give her away,"* Savannah's father stated while nodding and acknowledging Savannah's mother. *"Very well,"* the pastor said. Savannah's father lifted up Savannah's veil to give her a kiss. I shook his hand and gave him a hug and then he took his seat next to Savannah's mother. I took my place next to Savannah and the ceremony continued. The pastor proceeded and the time for the vows came. I started, *"I never thought I would fall in love again. I had a tragic moment in my life, but from that I have had many triumphant moments: us dating, getting engaged, our daughter Serenity and now here pledging my love to you in front of our family and friends. I know we will have plenty more triumphant moments together and I look forward to spending the rest of my life with you."* I kissed Savannah's hand and told her that I loved her. Savannah had a smile with tears in her eyes the whole time. *"Sincere I love you. You are a great man and a great father; you stood for me when I did not have the strength to stand for myself. You refused to let me go even when the doctors told you there was no hope. I look forward to spending the rest of my life with you."* Savannah kissed my hand back. The pastor blessed the wedding rings and presented them. Savannah and I also pledged traditional vows and took communion together. The pastor then said, *"I now present to you for the first time in public, Mr. and Mrs. Sincere Robinson."* Everyone clapped and cheered. The wedding party stood outside of the church to take pictures, then it was off to the reception. Savannah, Serenity, and I were in the Jaguar limo. The wedding party was in a Cadillac limo together. Our parents shared a limo along with

Savannah's grandmother. We all arrived at the reception hall and the D.J. announced Savannah's grandmother, our parents, the wedding party and finally Savannah and me. Our first dance was to "You Are" by Charlie Wilson. It was like Savannah and I were the only two people in the room while we were dancing. We just danced and stared into each other's eyes. Savannah interlocked her fingers behind my neck while I held her waist. I kissed her soft beautiful lips and told her that I loved her. She told me she loved me and smiled. Once dinner was finished and everyone was dancing, Savannah and I snuck out for a minute. We went to the "Sun Room." It's a room in the reception hall that was full of windows. We stood by the window holding each other watching the sunset. She turned to me and kissed me. The photographer must have saw us sneaking out because he was able to take a picture of us kissing with the sun setting behind us. Savannah and I heard the picture being taken and started laughing. *That was a perfect shot; you will thank me for it I promise.* We all started laughing and headed back to the reception hall. We made it back just in time to cut the cake and we enjoyed the rest of the night with our family and friends. At the end of the reception, Savannah and I thanked everyone for coming. Savannah and I gave her parents Serenity's car seat and we kissed every-one. We took a photo with Serenity and we kissed her. Savannah and I changed clothes and then headed to the airport.

"Mrs. Sincere Robinson, wow we did it Sincere," Savannah said looking up at me. *"Yea babe, we did,"* I said with a smile. We were on a private jet on the way to our honeymoon in Aruba. We arrived in Aruba where I carried Savannah across the threshold and laid her on the bed. After taking showers, Savannah and I made love for the first time as husband and wife. We fell asleep holding each other. I finally got it. Cyan told me while she was dying, *"I love you Sincere, you will be fine I promise you."* She was right. I wondered if she saw this day. She kept her promise. I looked at Savannah and looked at our wedding rings. I thought about Serenity and our families. I thought about everything that happened from the time I reached Virginia until now and thought to myself, you're right Cyan, I am fine.

Note from the Author

Ladies, there are men in the world who love their woman and can stay committed, no matter what temptations come their way. Believe me, they have help resisting the temptation.